Stealing Heart

Robbie Richmond

Contents

~ Chapter 1 ~

Why can't I be a raven?

Ravens are so pretty

They're free

No responsibilities, but full of opportunities. I assume it must be a good feeling. The beautiful bird could be anywhere it wanted to, yet it sits on the window seal of my french class. Who am I to judge? Maybe it's fun for the birds to watch my unraveling as I watch theirs.

I guess I've never asked a bird

"Miss Beckette."

The bothersome voice of my french teacher tears my eyes away from the birds. Ms. Boucher looks at me expectantly, tapping her foot as she normally does when she waits for someone to answer.

"Yes?" I quirk a brow at her.

Are we really going to do this every time? I have the whole scene mapped in my brain. She taps her foot three times, then asks the question again.

Once I give an answer or tell her I don't know, she'll let out a small sigh and shoots me a piercing gaze.

Sometimes she'll even mutter a smart remark as she walks away

"How do you formally ask for someone's name?" She mocks my brow movement, creating one of her own.

"Comment vous appelez-voucher."

I'm not dumb, you're class is just boring

"Tres bien." She sighs, like I knew she would, and turns away.(Very well)

I swear it takes effort to be such a bitch

I check the clock; there are still thirty minutes left. I look back over at the window hoping to still see the pretty raven. Much to my dismay, the bird is no longer there.

Sad

<3

"Why don't you just switch out of her class?" My best friend, Olivia, comments after I tell her about the interaction with my french teacher earlier this morning.

"It's not that easy, Liv." I sigh, sitting in my seat for our marine biology class. "My father would never let me quit french, plus, it's too late in the year."

My father is a very strict man, extremely shrewd at that. He has solid goals for me once I graduate, and that includes taking four years of french.

"I mean, I can stay after school and help you study today." She suggests, pulling out her binder.

"Really?"

"Yeah, I mean, I need to study for my-"

"Yo!"

Olivia is cut off by some boy in the back of our class, "My friend thinks you're cute."

He gestures to a kid behind him. His friend rolling his eyes. I look back at the boy who spoke. Boys seem to never change, not in highschool at least. I don't know what they get out of messing with people. I'll have to ask one.

"You're a senior?" I deadpan, "Shouldn't you leave the kiddie shit in middle school."

I hate boys

"Shoot, my fault." He turns back to his friends as they laugh and cut up in the back of the class.

"Vic, don't you know who that is." Olivia hits my shoulder.

I shake my head.

"That's Kaiden Smith's little brother."

"So?" I look at her blankly.

"Kaiden Smith is fucking hot."

Classic Olivia move

"What is Kaiden's little brother doing in our Bio class anyway?" I glance over my shoulder. Looking a little closer at him now, he does resemble his brother quite a bit. Blond with blue eyes, a dazzling smile.

"Apparently he's some sort of genius, plus they're like eleven months apart. Irish twins, I think is what it's called,"

I scoff, "He sure doesn't act like some genius."

Who was I to talk? I was technically a junior, but this year would be my last. It is expected of me to walk the stage with graduates this year. I'm excited, to say the least. Once I finish school I'll leave home, maybe try to figure out what I want to do.

Not what my father wants me to do.

"Speaking of Kaiden Smith," Olivia presses her shoulder against mine, a stupid smirk plastered on her face. I bite back a smile.

"I'm not going to his party Friday," I know Olivia too well.

She rolls her eyes, "Come on,"

"Do you remember the last party we went to?" I whisper, trying to pay attention to our teacher.

I think if I get fussed at again today; I just might cry.

"You and Mia got drunk out of your minds." I shoot her a pointed look, "I had to pull you away from a guy once it was time to leave. Then you puked all on my new shoes!"

"It's not like you can't afford new ones, in fact, you probably asked your dad for the same pair."

Sting

I hate when she does that, she does it often. I don't think she means for her words to cut deep. If truth be told, she most likely meant it as a joke. I'm just sensitive to the topic, I can't blame her for not knowing. She wouldn't get it.

"Whatever," I mumble, placing my focus on the teacher again.

"Bottom line you're going. I won't drink this time. I'll even be DD."

DD = Designated Driver

That, she will absolutely not be

"Alright, class is dismissed but don't forget about your test-" My teacher's voice fades as I make my way out of the door.

"Ugh, I love Mrs. Right but her voice is so droning,"

I chuckle.

"She almost makes it too easy to fall asleep in her class," I add.

It was Wednesday, an indication that the week was almost over but it feels like it's just started. I want to cry, but I also wanted to hit something.

You know? It's just one of those days.

The library smelled marvelous. The sweet, musky scent is something only a true book lover could appreciate. I always equated the smell of a library to vanilla beans. Fresh vanilla beans, straight from the earth.

"Bonjour!" I smile brightly at the librarian, she shoots me a wink. (Hello!)

This isn't the first time I've had to come into the library to study for a french test. She apparently took french in high school, although she couldn't help me with anything she was really good company.

"Do you even know her name?" Olivia chuckles as we find a place by the large window to sit.

"Nope," I move my gaze, "But that's not important, she's actually really cool."

I pull out my textbook, flipping through the unfamiliar words. The idea of being able to speak another language was great. I would love to be bilingual, at the same time it's easier said than done.

Olivia took Spanish so she can't help me, yet I do appreciate her willingness to stay a study with me.

The library doors bust open, I quickly shift my eyes towards it. A frown etched my face. People have always treated the library like a zoo. Don't get me wrong, I don't care. Just don't do it while I'm trying to study.

Ms. Boucher stomps in. A group of boys following in after her. Olivia gasps, I raise a brow at her.

"You know them?"

Looking closer, one of the boys seemed to be Kaiden Smith. There were four of them in total. I'm sure I've seen them around school before, I just haven't taken notice of them until now.

"Vic, it's Axel Stone." She breathes.

"He's back."

~ Chapter 2 ~

"**B**ack from what?"

She's being very dramatic.

"Rumor has it, his parents sent him to some military school because he's been in gang-related activity." I looked a little harder at the boy she gestured at.

What she said was probably not true. Not that I think she meant to lie, I just think you have to take every rumor with a grain of salt. As well as I just don't care what these boys are into. It has nothing to do with me.

I'd be lying if I said the boy wasn't attractive. He very much was. I don't know if it was the light gray eyes or those sharp feature of his, but something about him was so...enticing.

As if he felt my gaze his eyes turned and met mine. His face had no expression, yet he still held eye contact.

I was-

Drawn

-to him

For the lack of a better expression.

The worst part is I can't tell what he's feeling. I decided to look away first, which was not something I'm accustomed to. I'm no stranger to flirting with boys and rule #1 is never look away first.

This time, however, I felt if I didn't look away we'd just continue to start at each other. Even though I couldn't read his expression I knew he didn't seem like the type to back down.

I shot Olivia a look to stop staring. I didn't want to embarrass myself more than I had already. We look down at our books as the librarian and Ms. Boucher talked. Loudly, may I add. I tried not to be nosy, I really did. They just made it so easy to hear.

"You're going to have to take these heathens."

Damn, heathens? Tell us how you really feel.

While I'm nose deep in the french textbook that I can't even understand. I felt more eyes on me. I didn't dare look back up at them. Ignoring them was the best possible plan right now.

"Where am I going to put them, Darcy?" That was Ms. Boucher's first name.

"Not my problem, the detention room is being occupied at the moment but these boys cannot get out of their punishment." Darcy goes on a rant, "Lord knows they'll just do it again."

They were going to do it again anyway, ma'am, whatever it is they did. Yelling at them and putting them in a room for three hours has zero effect on their behavioral issues.

"No."

"I wasn't asking."

That was the last thing Ms. Boucher said before storming out of the room. There was a moment of complete silence. I finally look up from my textbook to share a look with Olivia. Her eyes saying that she was thinking the same thing I was thinking.

What. The. Fuck.

"Sit in the corner boys." The librarian sighed, "Just wait until the hours are done and be quiet."

I felt bad for my librarian friend. It was a hard time for anyone who wanted to go against Ms. Boucher. I don't even know why they still have her around. I haven't seen anyone have an 'A' in her class. Even the students that are fluent in French have a hard time in her class.

I let curiosity get the best of me as I turned to face the pair of eyes that were on me.

Axel Stone

Only this time, a prominent smirk sat on his lips. I took the time to look at his clothing. He didn't seem like a bad boy, not just by look at his clothing at least. It was his aura that presented him as trouble. The way he carried himself, I couldn't think straight.

"Should we leave?" Olivia asked I turn back around. I thought about it.

"Are you done?"

She nods.

"Then yeah, let's head out."

I gather my belongings, going very slowly as I still felt his eyes on me. They made me shiver. I didn't like it. What was special about him? What's the difference between him and any other guy I've had an attraction to?

Before making my way to the door, I looked back at him with a sigh. He wasn't directly staring at me this time, but best believe as soon as I looked at him his eyes were back on mine. This time his head was tilted in curiosity.

I give him a once over, then a light smile.

<3

I pull into my driveway and just sit. I don't want to go in.

I was just enjoying my life; it seems like I have two now. The Victoria at school and the Victoria at home are completely different people. I get out of my car, locking the door.

"Hello?" I yell into the large house.

My father is usually working late when I come home from school. Today I was home a little later because of the library. Not that he would care.

"You're home later than usual." His voice rang through the kitchen as soon as I walked in; startling me.

"I was at the library," I state, my tone dead.

"You say that every time, Victoria." My father's voice was stern, as it always is when he speaks to me.

I love my father and I know he still loves me

"And I'm there every time, Father." I hold an urge to roll my eyes, I'm not stupid. "I thought you were working late on the campaign tonight. You said you were last weekend."

He took a sip of his drink before returning his eyes to his computer, "I'm not."

I nod silently, ending the conversation there. There was honestly no point in trying to talk to him anymore. He was playing a character for his job and I was a part of the play. We all were. I'm supposed to be the perfect daughter and he's supposed to be a loving father.

As you can see he doesn't play his character very well

I take myself upstairs. He calls me again.

"I'm taking your mother to dinner tonight, we won't be back for a while."

Ah, my mother

At this point, I couldn't even be resentful towards her anymore. She and my father, I believe, have never been in love. They dated in high school, my mother got pregnant, and in a small southern town like this one. You face up to your mistakes and get married. I guess that's one of the reasons why I'm an only child.

I lock my bedroom door. Sighing as I sit by my window. I like doing this. It's the only thing I enjoy really. It's my own form of symbolism you could say.

I often sneak out to go to a park from my childhood. That neighborhood is abandoned now so no one goes there.

My home life hasn't always been so bland. My parents use to get along, tolerate each other. This hidden tension began once my father started his campaign. Specifically the affair with his campaign manager.

It's disgusting how he doesn't even try to hide it. He comes home smelling of expensive perfume and sex. The lipstick stains on his collar seem as if he's parading them around.

My mom is a closeted alcoholic, but at least she doesn't drink in front of me. She tries to hide it. In my sixteen years of living, I've seen more liquor bottles in that woman's closet than in my entire life.

I shake my head, there's no need to dwell on the things I can't control. I'll get out of here one day.

Just wait

~ Chapter 3 ~

I woke up late

Like really late.

So late that if I didn't think my father was going to kill me, I would have just skipped the day. My parents came home at about three-forty in the morning. They were arguing very loudly. What it was about wasn't important, but it seemed to go on forever. That was until I heard a loud noise and everything stopped. The next sound was footsteps and a door slam.

I should've gone down, I should've gone to see what the noise was. The truth is, I was scared. A part of me knew what the sound was. I know what a skin on skin slap sounded like. I hated the thought of my father putting his hands on my mother. I was still holding onto some type of humanity to be in him.

That all left last night

I no longer want to keep a relationship with my father when I leave. I'm still thinking about my mother though.

I quickly got dressed and did my morning pleasantries. I subconsciously put a little more effort into my outfit. I wanted to be noticed, as childish as that sounds. I didn't yearn for a conversation.

However, I can't deny that I wanted his attention again.

I give myself one last look in the mirror, then rush out of the house. If I floor it, I can make it to school in five minutes. I've already missed first period and the beginning of second. I haven't even entered the student parking lot and can already tell it's going to be a long day.

But, shit, at the same time, isn't every day?

I decided to just sit out on second period instead of getting a tardy. Three tardies equal detention and my father would go into cardiac arrest if he found out I had served a detention. Besides three years of highschool have taught me if you're going to be late, be really late.

I lock my car, heading to the back of the school. It was an unspoken rule that if you were late or skipping. You would enter or exit through the back entrance of the school. Some kid on the admin roll set that up for us my freshman year. He will truly be a legend.

The smell of cigarette smoke floats through the air as I round the corner. I almost pause as I see the group of boys hanging out by the entrance. People normally didn't hang out around the door.

The beautiful grey-eyed boy leans against the brick wall with a cigarette resting lazily in his mouth. His eyes trail down my body, before maintaining eye contact with me again. I smirk internally at the choice of my outfit.

"Excuse me." I gesture to the door that Axel Stone seemed to be perched against.

"Door's locked, Princess." He exhales smoke through the side of his mouth, making an effort for it not to go in my face

Such a gentlemen

"Bull," I ignore his choice of a nickname.

"Might as well sit here and chill with us," Another one of the boys' comments. He was sitting on an old box.

"That sounds amazing, but I'd prefer to go to class," I pressed my lips together, "Why is the door locked?"

Axel sneers at me, "How the fuck should I know?"

I quirk a brow at his new attitude, "Well, if you don't know then move so I can find out."

"I don't like being told what to do."

"I don't give a shit what you like."

I push Axel to the side, it wasn't hard but it did its job. I grab the crowbar that's hidden in one of the flower pots and open the door.

As I said, the boy who did this is a legend

"How-"

"Don't worry about it." I brush him off starting down the hallway.

I knew they weren't going in, they probably have no intention of going to class. My attraction to Axel didn't falter but my annoyance for him matched it. He was a dick. With that being said, he was a cute one and that was the problem.

<3

"Do you have a dress?"

The girls were talking about the party tomorrow. Everyone was excited, discussing dresses and color combinations. I wasn't dreading it, but I'm not exactly thrilled. All high school parties are the same, trust me, I've been to my fair share. I don't drink, but I do dance.

I normally have fun, but when I'm ready to go, I'm ready to go. That's something my friends don't understand.

My phone rings in my pocket, I quickly check the caller ID:

Father

I excuse myself from the table, walking to the small outside seating area. No one was out here because it's eighty degrees and humid in my lovely little town. I sigh deeply before picking up the call.

"I'm at school," I stated blankly.

"You were late,"

"Was I?"

"Victoria.." His voice was stern again, pure agitation evident in his voice.

"Did you need something?"

"If your grandfather is rolling in his grave right now. What the hell is wrong with you talking to me like that?" He spits into the phone.

"I've seen that you've lost your damn mine so I'll remind you that something bigger than you is on the line. I have a campaign to run, Victoria, I don't have time to baby you? My instructions aren't complicated or hard. You disappoint me every day, give me a fucking break."

"Fa-"

"I'm speaking," He snaps, "You forget yourself, child. Every single teen at that damned school dream of the life you've been born into. Stop acting like a damn brat. You get your ungratefulness from your mother."

He was right

I often think of how fortunate I am. I do not deny that I have the ideal teenage life. I never go without, I can thank my father for that. Yet, I'm still unhappy. I know I'm wrong for that. I am ungrateful, but how do I turn my feelings off?

"I understand,"

"We will discuss this further when I get home."

If I had anywhere to go, I'd run away

"Goodbye, Father."

I don't give him a chance to answer as I just hang up the phone. I couldn't go back to my table and fake a smile. My mood was absolutely crushed. I can see all the girls smiling from the window. I didn't want to bother them.

The feeling of something rolling down my cheek caught my attention:

A tear

I probably looked a mess. I quickly decided I would just text Olivia. Many excuses ran through my mind, none of them were good but again they didn't really have to be. The bottom line was, I'm not going back to lunch.

Hey, my dad called. I'll meet you in Bio, okay?

I shoved my phone back in my pocket, turning to walk back into the school through the front entrance.

Now this time, I did pause. As soon as I turn around I'm met with piercing grey eyes. They were certainly gorgeous; I have to wonder what kind of genes you're created with to be so fortunate. He was a beautiful man. If my pride wasn't so large I'd be at my feet for him; Axel Stone.

Axel Stone stood against his motorcycle. A Harley-Davidson deluxe in vivid black to be exact.

It was the exact same model I had begged my father for once I got my license. He, of course, said 'over my dead body' and I never brought it up again. I look at him expectantly, in return, he shakes his head. A smirk sitting on his lips.

"Need a ride, Angel?"

~ Chapter 4 ~

"**S**o do you, just like, not go to class?"

I roll my eyes, but nevertheless, walk over to where he stood.

"If I was in class, then I couldn't be your knight in shining armor." He smirks playfully at me, pushing off the bike to stand fully on both feet.

"More like bad boy in shining leather."

I take note of the classic black leather jacket he had on. On any other person, I would've eye-rolled at such a cliché outfit choice. Axel just made it looks so good.

He sported a plain black tee under the jacket and some dark jeans. Simple, yet breathtaking. He'd now shown me that he can look dazzling in any aesthetic. Seeing as yesterday he wore a sweatshirt and jeans.

He chuckles, "So you riding or not?"

I look again at his gorgeous motorcycle. It reminds me of how upset I was when my father said I couldn't have one. I would've bought it myself, but that wouldn't look good for my father's campaign so it's never been an option. I can only imagine the way she purrs.

"Scared? It's just a-"

"Deluxe, I know," I cut him off. I probably know more about this bike than he does. "She's so pretty."

I circle the bike. He took very good care of the bike. That internally made me happy.

"Here." He hands me a black helmet from the seat compartment of the bike.

I remember where we are. I remember who I am. I've already made my father upset about being late. I can only imagine what he would do if he found out I skipped.

However, I'm also furious, he controls every aspect of my life. The one time I do something outside of his schedule, he blows up on me. I am not my mother. I might put up with his shit, but I sure as hell won't make it easy for him.

"Is the goodie-two-shoes part of you starting to have it's way?" Axel taunts.

This wasn't peer pressure. I truly did not give a fuck about what Axel Stone thought of me. I was spiteful, craving for something selfish.

"No, I was wondering if I could drive?"

<3

He, in fact, did not let me drive.

It's okay though, riding on the luxurious bike has made my whole week. Axel was surprisingly very gentle with the ride. He avoided potholes, every once in a while he looked over his shoulder to make sure I was okay. He even asked if the speed was good.

We'd been driving for a long time, not that I noticed, I loved every minute of the ride. I couldn't actually tell you an exact time for how long we'd been on the road. I just can tell that when we left school it was light and when we stopped the sun was on the verge of setting.

"I have to say," He starts, "I'm impressed." Axel gets off the bike holding out a hand to help me off.

"Glad I could impress you." I retort.

He took me to some type of car show. It looked like a scene off of Fast and Furious. Pimped out cars scattered the open dirt area. I looked extremely out of place.

"Where are we?"

Axel doesn't answer, he just takes my hand in his and walks through a large crowd. The crowd seems to move for him. Maybe it was the hard face he had on or the confidence that oozed out of him, but no one would make eye contact with either of us. Axel nodded to a large man in black before walking through a door.

Axel's friends sat on the leather couch in the rather large office. They joked and laughed, then once Axel walked in they greeted him with a handshake. They turn their attention to me.

"Oh shit, it's one of the girls from the library," One of his friends laugh.

I give him a small wave looking back over to Axel. His hand was still connected to mine. I quickly drop it, despite the comfort I found from his large cold hands. They cooled my hot ones.

"Her name is Victoria, dumbass,"

I just realized that I hadn't told Axel my name, but I'm going to ignore how he knew it for now.

"I'm Tyler, sweetheart, nice to meet you," Tyler shoots me a lazy smile and a wave.

"Kaiden," I already knew that.

"Noah."

Noah smiles brightly at me, which I return. I think Noah's my favorite. Despite Noah's friendly composure, all of the boys in this room radiated authority. Not the presidential kind, but more like the steal your girl kind.

"You can sit next to me, pretty lady." Tyler smiles boyishly.

"Tyler..." Axel warns, before pulling me gently to a loveseat where he sits next to me. Tyler just chuckles to himself, shooting me a wink.

The boy's fall into a comfortable, light-hearted conversation. I didn't feel out of place, they made it very welcoming for me. With that being said I still couldn't help but feel a little lonely. This is the way friends were supposed to act with each other. I didn't have that. I absolutely love my girls and they're good to me.

As well as they're able, I suppose, but I couldn't count on them.

"Are you driving tonight?" Kaiden asked. I could tell there was a shift in energy around the room. A once playful vibe turned into a serious one.

"Yeah, the prize is going to be twelve thousand." I cock my head at Axel's response, yet I didn't ask any questions. He didn't answer me when I asked where we were. He probably wasn't going to tell me what he meant, so why bother?

"It starts in twenty minutes, I'll let Romano know." Noah treads out of the door.

"What are you going to do with her?" Kaiden gestures to me, he's very standoffish towards me. It's probably because I insulted his brother.

His brother's a child in a teen's body

Axel shifts his gaze to me, "You'll watch her in the seeing booth."

I frown softly. I did not want to be left alone. Normally if you take a girl with you somewhere, you have intentions of staying there with her the whole time. Not leaving her with people she barely knows. He's lucky I have no real goals in life, or else I'd have a real problem with the situation.

I pull on his jacket slightly, "You're not leaving me alone, are you?"

I make my voice low so only he can hear. I didn't want to offend Kaiden or Tyler.

"The race won't last long, you'll have eyes on me the entire time."

Race?

It started to click: The dirt roads, the bodyguards, Axel's nice ass motorcycle. I was at a fucking drag race. I stand and throw open the door. The sign we passed had the name of the track, but I was too occupied to read it.

Devil's Way

I was all too familiar with this track. My father absolutely despises the underground scene. His main goal in the campaign is to get rid of this track specifically. He's been preparing his speech for when he announces he's running for Mayor later this year. This track's name is laced throughout the entire thing.

I- I can't be seen here

I stomp back in the room, "Did you know?"

"Know what-"

"Don't play with me, asshole, did you know about my father? Is that why you brought me here?" I'm glaring at everyone in the room.

"About him running for Mayor? Yeah, so?"

My jaw ticks.

"Take me back," I demand.

"No."

"Axel,"

How could I be so stupid? Why would I ever think he would be so nice out of nowhere. Yeah, a hot boy just randomly offers you a rid, Victoria, smart thinking.

"They need you down there, the fight starts in ten." Noah walks into the room, clearly unaware of the tension. I didn't mean to glare at him, but it's not something I could just turn off.

"Wait, what's wrong?"

~ Chapter 5 ~

Noah's question went unanswered,

I was beyond upset. Partly at myself, I know he's not one to follow rules. Yet, I hopped on his bike and followed him up. This was only my fault. Letting my emotions get ahead of rationale; I could hear my father's voice.

"Do your dumbass race, then take me back to school." Is the only thing I said to Axel.

I follow behind Kadien as we walk up some stairs into an all room where the walls were fully glass. It was an overlook at the track. You could see all the obstacles from this room. I, unfortunately, could see Axel's beautiful self and bike from here. I would've sat down with the boys, but I was mad at them too.

I could feel the paranoia and anger seeping out of my pores. Why the fuck am I here? I met this boy when he was serving detention, then decided to hop on a bike with him. Him and his dumbass friends. I hope he falls off his bike...

They all were probably in on it; maybe had some strong vendetta against my father and wanted to take it out on him, through me. Little did they know, I was going to have to be the one to go through the consequences, not them.

I could hear them whispering, no doubt about me. I didn't care though. Let them talk. They weren't speaking anything of importance to me. I had one thing on my mind:

Get. Home.

I didn't even want to check my phone, I was petrified. My heart was pounding outside of my chest. I only noticed how bad my father scared me when I did something wrong. Last night only re-illustrated why. If he could hit my mother, he could hit me.

"Calm down, Victoria, Axel didn't mean you any harm." I don't know which one said it, as my back was to them, but I didn't care. I kept quiet.

They needed to start the race soon so I could get my car and go home.

"Can you at least sit down, Axel would kill me if you passed out."

Shut. Up.

"I'll walk back to school myself if you don't stop talking to me," I state wrapping my arms around myself. The boys stay quiet.

The race starts, eight bikes that I counted sped through the track. Dirt was kicked everywhere, no doubt smoking out the people watching from below.

"Oh, shut the hell up." A female voice entered the room. This causes me to turn my head away from the race. She was very pretty, with long raven black hair, striking green eyes. Confidence followed her, unlike everybody else I had met today.

Confidence seemed to envy her

She pauses when she sees me, "You kidnapped another girl? This one's pretty."

She smiles. I manage to smile back at her.

"This one came willingly," Tyler snorted.

I grab a water bottle off of a close table and throw it at him. He's getting on my nerves.

"Suck on it, maybe it can keep you quiet for a second," I mumble turning back around.

My eyes immediately are drawn to Axel's. I could see his eyes through the helmet. They were intense. This time I don't look away, wanting to challenge him. A bump was coming up, yet his eyes were still on mine. I was weary.

Even though I was upset at him, doing a jump with looking was basically suicide. Especially with him in first place.

He did it. Flawlessly, in fact, twisting sideways in the air. I hide my surprise, staring at him for only a few more moments then looking at some of the other riders.

"Show off," A voice states from behind me.

I snort, quickly covering it with my hand before looking at the person next to me. It was the girl. She was giggling along with me.

"I guess you could say that," I smile softly.

"I'm Athena," She smiles, offering me her hand.

I shake it.

"Victoria."

Axel finishes his last lap. Winning first place. They hand him an envelope and then escort him somewhere. My annoyance increases as I think about seeing him again.

"Axel is nowhere near as cool as he portrays himself to be," She laughs.

"Good to know," I start to leave before she calls me back.

"I'll give you my number, call me whenever he bothers you again," I smile, actually liking this girl. We exchange numbers, turns out she actually goes to our school.

But she's a hardass like the boys and barely shows up.

"Ready?" I automatically roll my eyes at the sound of Axel's voice.

I turn to meet him. He throws the envelope to Kaiden, locking his eyes back with mine. I nod a simple goodbye to Athena before pushing past Axel to get through the door.

It seemed like even more people crowded around than earlier. Axel quickly catches up with me, grabbing my hand again. I snap my head towards him, trying to pull my hand out of his grip. He only wraps his arm around my waist, guiding me towards the bike.

He was trying to get me to kill him.

"Axel, if you don't let me go you're going to never get the chance to have kids," I grit out.

His face is still solid, void of emotion as he speaks to me.

"You're in a very dangerous place, with very dangerous people. Put your emotions aside. we'll fight later,"

God he fucking irks me

I looked like a little kid, pouting as he led to his bike. It might have looked cute to an outside viewer, but to me? I was angry. Shaking from words that I wanted to say and express but regardless keep to myself.

I still have to get a ride to my car

<3

As soon as he stopped in the dark school parking lot I hopped off of the bike and started towards my car. I'd refused to put a helmet on simply because he offered it. I wanted nothing to do with him. Besides, because of him, I was about to be in a world full of pain.

"Victoria,"

This had been the first time he used my name, I was so shocked it caused me to pause.

"I knew about your father, but I didn't ask you to go along with me because of that. I didn't even connect the dots,"

Honestly, whether tonight was planned or not was none of my concern anymore. I was strictly concerned about getting home.

I turn to face him, opening my mouth to say something before realizing there wasn't anything to say. I settle for a nod of understanding. Quickly getting into my car and pulling out of the parking lot. I saw Axel's bike lights still on in the parking lot, he was still there.

I finally allow myself to check the clock

11:36

Oh my fucking god

I wasn't even going to explain myself. I wasn't going to tell him where I was and I wasn't going to make up a lie. I was going to take whatever news he had to give me and my punishment. It was the best way I could see this going.

I got home in record time: three minutes. I jumped out of my car, barely locking the door. I silently creep through my front door. Seeing the kitchen light on, I knew he was up. He was up and not happy.

I walk through the kitchen, already on the verge of tears.

"Victoria," His voice was scarily calm.

I didn't say anything, but I faced him. In the kitchen, it was my mother, the campaign manager, and my father. Something in my gut told me what was going on. My mother, unlike she usually does, was drinking straight out of a wine bottle. She was gone. I don't even know if she knew where she was.

"Where have you been?"

Silence

He raises his eyebrow at me, "I asked you a question, child, where the hell have you been?"

I refused to look at anybody else but him. Even if I had an excuse, I couldn't speak, if I even moved to open my mouth a wail would come out. Crying would only make the situation worse.

"If you don't start acting right, I'm going to have to kick you out. I will not put up with a rebel." He begins.

"I'm not sure what's going on with you, but cut it the hell out. I don't have time to deal with your rebellion. If you think I won't ship you off to some boarding, you're dead wrong. You have privileges and you have responsibilities."

When my father gets angry, there's this vein that pops out in his forehead.

"I understa-"

"Then stop being a bitch."

If I was close enough, I would've felt the spit leaving his lips. He always speaks to me so harshly. As if I'm one of his employees and not his daughter. His only daughter at that.

"What did you need to tell me?"

I was bold, too bold

My father got this look in his eye. It was concerning. His blue eyes constricted, a glare morphed into them. A glare meant for me. He seemed so infuriated with me.

"Your mother and I are getting a divorce."

~ Chapter 6 ~

I should've seen it coming

I knew they weren't happy. Yet, I'm still stunned. The worst part is, last night should have been the last straw for my mother. I would love to think she grew a backbone and initiated the divorce. However, I know this was my father's idea. It was all on his accord.

I sit on the cold stone of my balcony, staring into the dark sky. It was empty, different from a usual starlit night. This would have been one of the nights that I'd sneak and go to the park. Where I'd cry and get everything out of my system.

But I was tired, physically and emotionally.

I want to sleep but my mind races. Did I put up with all this shit just for them to get a divorce? Why didn't they get it sooner then? Maybe I'm being selfish, my parents are miserable together. This could be a good thing. No-shit- wait- my father wouldn't let me live with my mother. I'll be staying with him.

The night air is strong. It whistles against the trees, embracing my skin. My emotions make me hot and the universe calms me down. I welcome the contrast, I need something to ground me. Something that reminds me that there is another world outside of my head, outside of my overwhelming thoughts.

Love seems like such an amazing complex.

The feeling of being totally involved with someone and them returning the feeling has to be one of mankind's favorite fairy tale. How does anyone expect me to believe in love if I've never seen it? My parents just might be living proof that love isn't real.

But I want it to be

I read stories, I understand the emotions that the characters feel. In my weakest moments, I imagine what it would be like to be able to tell some-one everything. Them understanding it and wanting to work through it with me.

Where's my prince charming?

Where's my happy ending?

<3

I sat in my car forty-five minutes before the bell rang. I got up earlier so I didn't have to see anyone. That includes my friends. I couldn't ignore them all day, but I sure couldn't feign happiness. Not today.

Shit!

It's Friday

The party

Oh. My. Fucking. God.

I slam my hand on the steering wheel. I want to go back home and crawl into a tiny ball. Then, I'm going to throw myself off of a cliff.

Of course, it's Friday.

Of course, there's a party today.

Of course, I agreed to go to it.

Last but not least, of course, it's Kaiden Smith's party.

Cars slowly start to fill the parking lot. People laughing and walking inside with their friends. Totally unaware of the small breakdown I'm having in my car. I try to look on the positive side. Maybe a night of careless dancing is something I need.

Yeah, still don't feel better-

I sigh, hopping out of my car. I start my way inside, already thinking of an excuse to leave the group. I smile and wave to passing acquaintances. Keep conversations small and sweet. No one noticed and no one cared. Which is fine, even if someone asked, I wouldn't tell them.

"Lost?"

"No, I'm pretty sure the best runaway route is this way. I appreciate your concern, though." I don't dare look into the eyes staring at the back of my head. I continue to walk.

"I hate to see you go, but I love to watch you leave," I can hear the smirk in his voice.

"Please, go to hell,"

"And you leave you here all alone?"

I turn around to face him, pausing in the now deserted hallway. He'd followed me all the way to the three hundredth hall. Everyone was in the commons.

"Such a pretty mouth to be wielding such hurtful words," He leaned against the lockers, looking devilishly handsome as always. I would've swooned over him if he didn't get on my goddamn nerves so much.

"Can you go be stupid somewhere that's away from me?" Despite the annoyed act I put on. This light conversation was probably what I needed. I would smile if my ego wasn't so big. I couldn't deny that talking to Axel made my day a little better.

"What's in it for me?" He was not longer smirking, a genuine smile plastered his face. I'd just noticed his dimples. They were light but extremely adorable. His eyes were playful.

"Are you flirting? Or trying to start a fight?"

"Eh, a little bit of both."

He was close, his hand gripped around my upper arm. I could feel his breath fan my face, he smelled of mint and tobacco, a faint lingering scent of his cologne, as well. A dangerously intoxicating smell.

I could only wonder what he tastes like

"That's too bad."

With the little restraint I had left, I pulled back. A smirk parading on my face. He seemed fulfilled by our banter too.

I walk into french, a smile still very prominent on my face. Not even Ms. Boucher could wipe it off.

"Good morning class, you have a surprise test today based on the notes you took yesterday."

Nevermind.

"What's going on with you?" Olivia starts as soon as I take my seat next to her.

My eyes drift to the back of the room. Kaiden's brother already looking at me. I have no doubt that he was at the track yesterday. I just hadn't seen him, but I'm sure he either saw me or his brother told him I was there.

"What are you talking about?"

I'd purposefully ignored her phone calls and skipped out on lunch today. I just couldn't take her condescending jokes, not today.

"You've been avoiding me, you've been avoiding all of us. "

"Wasn't avoiding you. I don't have my phone." I explain, "What did you need?"

"Well, I was just wondering what color dress you were going to wear? We can't wear the same color-" She goes off on a tangent, her concern no longer there. Just like I knew it wouldn't be.

Truth was, I hadn't even thought about the party since it was last mentioned. I'd forgotten completely about it. Unlike her, I hadn't planned the party to be the highlight of my life. Once I got home, I would pick a random dress out of my closet. Throw whatever makeup I feel like on. Then call her to say I was on my way.

"Y'all are going to the party?"

I turn around, it was Kaiden's brother who asked. It's kind of sad that I still don't know his name. I nod.

"Oh, this is going to be fun."

~ Chapter 7 ~

My father wasted no time kicking my mother out

All of her stuff was on the front porch when I got back to school. By all of her stuff, I mean ten dollars and a bottle of tequila. Another part of my father's campaign was 'protect your family and provide' meaning my mother couldn't work for all sixteen years they were married.

"Mom?" I slow as I gaze at her state.

She wasn't drunk, she was crushed.

"Hi, baby." She tries to smile, but it comes across as a sad look. I run to hug her.

"It's alright, mama." I shake my head, "You didn't lose anything important. The man in there has changed, but he has given you a gift. Maybe you can go start your life now."

False confidence creates real confidence

"Your father wants full custody,"

I knew that already

I nod, "I graduate soon, then I'll ask to be emancipated,"

"Your father would never let that get in the news,"

"He won't have a choice," I smile softly, "Don't worry about me. I'm fine."

A honk brings me away from my mother, "That's my ride."

Before she gets in she takes hold of my face, "Be careful baby, don't let him get to you."

"Get clean, mom." She wipes away a tear that slipped past my eye. At this moment, I realized how much I truly resented my father. I'd never met such a selfish person. He was probably going to bring that bitch in to replace my mother.

I also hold some sort of resentment towards my mother. She's the best at giving comforting words after the damage is already done. She can't protect herself and she's never tried to protect me. She's always been okay with doing the bare minimum - just enough to get by. Maybe that's how she settled with my father in the first place.

It's wrong - to feel like she failed in protecting me. However, I stand here watching her walk away from me without much of a fight. She clutches her tequila bottle in her hand harder than she's ever hugged me.

I get he hurt you but I'm your daughter-

Once my mother's cab pulls away, I stomp into the house. Heading straight for the stairs, I wanted to make all kinds of trouble tonight.

"Victoria." My father's stern voice echos through the large stairwell. I keep walking. I pick the tightest dress I can find and throw it on.

Fuck everyone, tonight

I pick my phone:

"Hello?"

"Come on, bitch, we have a party to go to"

<3

The music was loud but the stench of weed was louder. My ears thumped to the rhythm of the current song. A smile etched my face walking in. Almost as soon as I crossed the door, my friends were scattered. However, today, I didn't care. I wasn't going to drink, but I sure as hell was going to dance.

I grab some random boy and pull him to the dance floor. Moving my hips along with the music, loving the way his hands felt on them. The smoke in the air with no doubt giving me a second-hand high.

I wanted to create hell tonight

"Excuse me-" A deep voice spoke behind me. "You're Axel's girl, I respect that."

Before I could tell the fine gentlemen I was dancing with that I was indeed, not Axel's girl; he was gone. I shrugged, dancing by myself.

I was erratic, swaying back and forth to a song I'd never heard before. I started dancing with some girl. She was pretty, really pretty. I was in a secret search for new friends and I was going to have to put her name on the list.

"Hey, my name's Blaze!" The girl yells over the music.

Blaze, very cool name

"Victoria, nice to meet you!" I laugh, shaking her hand.

After a few more songs, we got bored and went into the kitchen. A makeshift bar was set up. Blaze goes up and hugs someone. When they turn around I almost gasp.

"Athena?" I smile, "Aren't I lucky to see you?"

She pulls me in for a hug, "I'm the lucky one, babe,"

"You want a drink?" She gestures to the bar, it seems that she was bartending tonight.

"No, I'm not drinking." I wave her off, "They have you bartending?" I joke.

"Yeah, Kaiden says I'm the best in the game."

I decide not to question how she knows Kaiden. I don't want to overstep my welcome. The girls were funny, joking about anything and everything. We were talking about the race last night until I heard my song play in the living room. I smile widely.

"We've had a long enough break!" I pull both girls into the living room.

The feeling of music coursing through my veins hits me again. I will admit, I like to dance, but I'm not very good at it. In moments like these, it doesn't really matter.

"The hottie behind you is staring," Blaze whispers in my ear as the song passes. I frown, turning around.

Sure enough, grey eyes were staring right back. Although I couldn't tell what they were thinking. I didn't care, I wink back at Blaze.

"I'll be back ladies."

Walking over to Axel I slowly lose my confidence, but I would never let him know. He was sitting on a couch with his friends. Kaiden's brother was there as well, a knowing smirk place on his stupid little face. When I get there I find myself a seat on Axel's lap. Reaching my arm around his neck.

I let a small smile set on my face as I leave a soft kiss on his neck. "Is there a reason why you were staring at me?"

Axel ignores my taunting question, "What are you doing here?"

"Having fun,"

"Dressed like that?" I pull away from his neck, cocking a brow.

"Problem?"

"Yes,"

"Good. Let's fix it."

"Victoria..." He warns. I had no intention of giving anything to him tonight, but why waste an opportunity to mess with him. I roll my eyes, standing up. His friends were quiet, looking at the scene unfold. I wink before heading upstairs. I pass the girls on the way there.

"I have to go handle something," I smile, "Keep the dance floor warm for me!"

I leave the door of the bedroom unlocked, knowing Axel would barge in any moment. I was ready for a fight today. I'm in tip-top shape to argue.

"What the hell are you trying to prove?"

"I have nothing to prove to you," I spin around to face him.

"Do you have any idea the looks you were getting from boys?" He was angry, but he looked so good.

A vein popped in his neck, drawing my attention to a tattoo I'd never seen before.

"No, and I don't care,"

"You need to leave." Axel takes off his jacket throwing it on me.

"Make me," I spit back.

He snorts, "You think you can just run that pretty mouth of yours whenever you want, huh?"

"Yeah, that's exactly what I think," I take a step closer, challenging him.

"If I didn't find you so damn attractive right now, I'd actually be mad,"

"Yeah? How attractive am I, Axel?"

We were chest to chest, my breath mingled with his. We were so close if I just moved forward two inches out lips would touch-

"Are you flirting? Or trying to start a fight?" He mocks my words from earlier.

"I haven't decided," I brush my lips, against his jaw. Pulling back, sadly.

I was trying to start trouble, not ruin my life

At least not yet

"I'll catch you later," Before leaving the room I turn to face him, "Stone."

I couldn't wipe the smile off my face. I'd had so much fun tonight. The only thing I had to worry about was falling in front of people with my heels. I could still feel my pulse racing from my encounter with Axel.

I'd been the girl, I've always wanted to be in that moment:

Confident

Controlled

Sexy

Dangerous

I was all of that and more tonight.

I walk into the house, wanting to make lots of noise. I had to finish the night with a bang. My heels echoed against the marble flooring of the home. I slammed the door and waited.

"Victoria Amora Beckette, have you lost your damn mind," My father's voice came from upstairs.

"Hi."

He was stomping down the stairs at an ungodly pace. It's almost as if he flew. He was pissed, but so was I.

"Where the hell have you been this time? You were probably with that Stone boy, weren't you?"

I freeze, how the hell did he know that?

"Yeah, I've had you followed. I knew you would follow your mother's path. I will have no daughter of mine become some no good skank."

"A skank?" I seethe at him, "You've got to be fucking kidding me. My mother has been with one man her entire life. You are the one that cheated on her. You have no right to call anyone a skank."

I begin up the stairs, quickly realizing that there was a reason why no one argued with my father.

"Victoria, I'm not done talking to you!" I can hear the spit fall from his mouth, he was gritting his teeth incredibly hard. "You are to never see that boy again, do you understand me?"

I don't answer, just continuing to walk up the stairs. My father following quickly behind me.

"Victoria, answer your father don't be disrespectful."

I pause at that. That was the first thing this woman has ever said to me. My jaw ticks at her nerve. I turn to face the perfect couple. The woman has a look of accomplishment on her face.

"You might fuck my father, but you will never be my mother."

My cheek burns as my head is thrown to the side. It didn't hurt much, but my eyes water up regardless.

He slapped me

***

< Dress I imagined >

Chapter 8

"I hate you."

Whether I really meant it or not, I don't know. I know that I absolutely mean it in this moment. It takes a different kind of person to hit your own daughter out of annoyance. No matter how angry I am, I can't deny the little girl in me wanting my father to be sorry for what he'd done. I wanted him to chase after me as I stomped out of the house. I wanted him to beg for forgiveness after everything he's put our family through, for that man he's become.

That was never going to happen. I knew it. He knew it. The whore he lays with at night knew it.

That bitch is no better

She may have gasped when he hit me, but she didn't do anything. She would probably stay with my father just like my mother did. My father would obviously get tired of her. Maybe throw her around a bit before casting her aside.

I sniffled softly under the dark sky. I was quickly out of the house soon after the incident. If I stayed any longer I would've started to do something I'd regret.

I sigh, trying to calm myself down with the cool air. I had so much fun earlier tonight. A small part of me thought everything was going to be okay. That I was starting to get my life together. A childish assumption - I just believed that I'd become a new person, that I'd had a new awakening. It's silly, I know. Of course, my father has to remind me that he controls every aspect of my life.

How could I ever forget? I know who I am.

I wasn't paying mind to my surroundings. I just let my feet take me where they wanted. As soon as I set eyes on the old playground. I let the tears roll. My chest heaves as my hands trace the swing seat I'd always pick. Flashbacks of past memories and smiles flow in and out of my mind.

Things haven't ever been good, but they've always been simple.

I sit on the swing, the salty tears that fell on my face only irritated my stinging cheek. I've never had anyone to count on. My mother's always been emotionally unstable and my father's always been stubborn. That's the way it's always been.

I keep a lot to myself because it's hard to come across people who understand. I hate that I'm still hoping for a happy ending with all my family. How do you let go of your parent? Especially if they're still living. I know what I have to do. I just can't bring myself to do it.

What do you do when that happens?

How do you find the courage?

How do you let go?

Truth: You cannot change things by loving them harder.

I've already tried.

I wonder, if I died, who would leave flowers at my grave? I think I know the answer, but in efforts to protect myself, I won't voice it. I often think that if I acted like I wasn't hurting; then it wouldn't hurt. That doesn't work. I still feel very much hurt, I've only added the loneliness to it.

I try to stand, feeling like I was suffocating from the lack of air. My chest movements were erratic. It didn't help that tears were blurring my eyes from the already dark scene. My knees weaken, but before I can hit the ground large arms wrap around me. They pull me against a hard chest, holding me upright. I wasn't scared because I knew that familiar smell all too well.

"Victoria?" His voice is hushed, "What's wrong?"

I don't answer, just relaxing in his arms. He seems to understand as he doesn't speak for a while. He just holds me under the moonlight. Softly rocking back in forth, he coos into my hair. My crying comes to a slow halt and thought's begin to unfog.

"Are you going to tell me what upset you, baby?" He pulls his head back from me. His eyes immediately go to my cheek. I hadn't known it was that noticeable. If he could see it in such dim lighting, it was going to be a bitch to cover in the morning. "Who the fuck did that to your face?"

His voice was no longer calm, it had now come off harsh. It echoed through the deserted park. A quick thought came across my mind: What was he doing here? Axel didn't come off as the person to just go for midnight strolls through a playground, but who am I to judge? I guess I didn't either.

"It doesn't matter." I remove myself from his hold, he lets me.

"I'll be damned!"

"And what are you going to do about it, Axel? Beat him up?"

"That's a hell of a good start," He exasperated, I shake my head.

"Then what?" I look directly into his beautiful grey eyes, "Then everything goes back to the way it was. Me in my situations and you in yours?"

"Don't talk to me like that?" He utters.

I give him a pointed look, "Like what?"

"Like I don't care,"

"Do you?" I raise a brow, "Everyone cares, Stone. It's not about caring,"

He hesitates, "Then what are you expecting?"

"From you? Nothing. I don't want you to do anything, I don't want you to think about it anymore. I want you to continue as if this never happened." I back away from him, "I know I will,"

"You have a handprint on your face, yet you still can't pull that stick from your ass. I asked who hurt you-"

"And I told you to drop it!" I looked at him wildly. He was upsetting me. I had a feeling that soon there was going to be a turn in the conversation and someone was going to get hurt. Someone was going to say something they didn't mean.

"You just have to make everything so fucking difficult, huh?" Axel tugs at his roots. I look away from him.

"You don't want me to care? Fine." He throws his hands up, "Go back to the loser that hit you. Then next time you can cry in that large house of yours. In fact, Go wipe your tears with daddy's money, princess."

Bingo! It was me. I was the one that was going to get hurt.

I won't lie. His words cut deeper than Olivia's could ever. I couldn't help the tears forming in my eyes, but I fought like hell to not let them fall. Not yet, not while he was watching. I wanted to come back at him. I wanted to tell him, that I indeed, would wipe my eyes with hundred dollar bills tonight. However, my throat constricted.

"Fuck you." My voice comes out soft, not weak. It was meaningful just not loud. Axel's jaw unclenched. "Next time you see me, don't talk to me, okay?"

"I mean, it Axel." I push him, he doesn't move. "I might take shit from other people in my life, that is beyond my control, but this-" I gesture to him, "I will not take this from you."

"Just remember I didn't ask you to come over here and ask me what's going on. I didn't ask you to care. I especially didn't ask for your fucking judgment!" I seethe.

"You're right, I will go home to my big house. I'll go home and forget all about you."

~ Chapter 9 ~

A XEL'S POV

It's been three days

Three full days

I haven't talked to her or seen her since our argument. I could laugh at myself if I wasn't so upset. I tried to tell myself that Victoria was just a phase. I would soon remove those striking blue eyes from my conscience.

The reality was: I felt bad.

I should've never said anything to her. I should've just held her and kept quiet. Then when I fucked up, my ego didn't even allow me to run after her. It's just that my emotions were mixed. After the way, she left me high and dry at the party. Then to find her crying on an old swing set. My mind was in a haze and I was acting on pure instinct.

The sound of a chain-breaking catches my attention, "Shit!"

My punching bag was on the ground. I let out a few more colorful words before shoving the bag aside. I had a match tonight. It wasn't a big one, but I wasn't focused. My mind was elsewhere. I've been training since twelve-thirty when I realized Victoria had not planned on showing up to school today. I wanted to apologize to her. Even if I didn't end up apologizing I wanted to see her. Set eyes on her, make sure she was okay.

"Get your head right!" Romano's voice boomed from the overhead track. "I didn't bet on you for you to be distracted. You will pay if you lose tonight."

I fucking hate the grumpy bastard

But he was my boss and I had bills to pay. I don't even look at him as I sit on the bench to get water. I clench and unclench my jaw.

I just wanted to get a glimpse of her goddamnit! Just a look, then I'd be fine.

"What the hell is going on with you?" Kaiden asks, sitting next to me on the bench. Kaiden was the only other person out of the boys that fought. The rest kept to racing and other activities.

Tyler nudges him, "He's thinking about that girl."

I roll my eyes at them. I don't know how I managed to steer clear of the blue-eyed beauty all these years. I was definitely sure that I was aware of her presence a little more than she was of mine. Jace, Kaiden's brother, told us about a hot girl that handed him his ass a few days ago. He took a picture and sent it to us. He was shocked, never before having to deal with a girl getting testy with him.

Then we saw her in the library that same day. Now it seems we always cross paths. She infuriates me to the fullest extent, yet I still continue to go out of my way for her attention.

"I can't focus," I sigh, rubbing my face. "That was her last night."

We were there for a gathering, discussing the match that was to go on today. Kaiden was talking to a guy that had been giving us problems. That was the only reason we were there. Halfway through I heard soft sniffles. I originally thought it was a little girl, after all, we were at a playground. When I turned the corner I saw the silhouette of a female that I hadn't stopped thinking about. Even in the dark, I could recognize her.

"It was? What was wrong?" Noah's face etched in concern, I felt a spark of aggravation. I slowly back that feeling away. I know he didn't mean it like that and if he did I shouldn't care.

"She wouldn't tell me, then we got in an argument." I sigh loudly, again cursing myself for my actions the previous night.

"Bro, how do you go from giving her puppy eyes all night to arguing with her?" Tyler sits on the ground in front of me. He was exaggerating a bit with the puppy eyes part, but I won't deny - I most definitely was looking at her at the party.

I shake my head, I didn't want to talk about it.

"I need to fix that bag." I gesture to the bright red bag laying on the ground.

"The match is in forty-five minutes."

<3

"Stone."

I made my way to the middle of the ring. The mat already smelled like sweat and blood. The lights were low, the crowd was loud. The guy that was against me matched my physique. If I could get my fucking mind in the ring, the match would be over in ten minutes.

No matter how much I tried to ignore it or act like it wasn't happening. My eyes were still searching the crowd. They looked through all of the girls' faces, not satisfied. I knew she wasn't here. She'd never been here, so why was I now searching for her pretty blues?

The announcer shouted the signal.

The match had started

The guy punched me in my jaw immediately. I pushed all thoughts to the back of my head and let my anger rise. I retaliated by kicking the back of his knee. Punching him in the stomach, then his nose caught my knee.

There was only one rule: No rules.

He was fast, faster than me. However, I have more endurance than he has. He was new, throwing hard punches on the first round. I couldn't falt him, he wanted the fight to be over. I did too.

I had taken him to the ground, he was pinned. He weakly tried to brace himself for the punches. I actually felt bad for him. I was throwing punch after punch. His face started to make my knuckles hurt. I was silently praying he would pass out or tap out soon. The last punch must've hit him at just the right angle as he was out cold.

The ref pulled me off of him, holding my arm in the air. He was shouting encouraging words at the crowd as the poor boy was being carried out of the ring. The crowd's volume grew even louder if that was even possible. I couldn't help my eyes carrying over the crowd. Many faces, but none of them hers.

I collect my money, walking roughly into my changing room. The young boy threw a few pretty powerful punch to my ribs, I was now starting to feel it. My lungs are cramping, I didn't even know that could happen.

Packing up my stuff has to be the worst part of this. After every match, you have to pack your belongings when all you really want to do is go home. I tried not to glance at the mirror, I could feel the heat in my jaw. I knew it would leave some kind of bruise.

Maybe she'll ask about it-

That was dumb.

Why would she care?

The crazy thing is I would tell her the truth in a heartbeat, really anything to get her to talk to me again. The lovely banter we have can't end this soon, right? I let in and look at my jaw. It was pink with purple blotches. It wasn't bad just irritated, although, it would be leaving a bruise.

However, the colors of my jaw weren't what caught my attention.

It was the mesmerizing blue eyes in the mirror looking back at me

~ Chapter 10 ~

I was pissed

I have this deep resentment in my chest and I don't know how to get rid of it. I climbed through my window and locked my door. When the morning came I didn't leave the house until I heard my father's car leave the driveway.

The worst part is, I don't know what I want

When kids yearn to get out of their parent's house, whatever the reason may be, they normally have a goal they want to accomplish. I, however, don't even know if I want to go to college or not.

I was hurt

I don't know why I thought Axel would run after me. That must be the hopeless romantic in me, the romance that I've never seen in person. I do appreciate it though, it just pushes me to detach myself from him. I've seen what high school relationships do to my parents. I need to get my mind right, Axel isn't a part of that.

I need to learn to stop expecting so much out of people. It's not anyone's job to save me. It's not anyone's job to run after me. I yearn for someone to understand me- but no one ever will. I just need to get the fuck over it already.

Just... just get over it

No more expectations = no more disappointments

I finally rolled out of my bed and went to my bathroom, catching a glimpse of my cheek in the mirror. It was red, slightly puffy. If I'd gone to school it would be noticeable. People may have not asked about it but they would have noticed it. I turned on the shower. I feel dirty, littered with anger and it makes my chest heavy.

I need a relief

I had the entire weekend to myself. I didn't have to do anything. I had no obligations, nothing. This, unfortunately, led me to think about my father. When I came home Friday night after my fight with Axel. He was gone. Him and his little rent-a-bitch. I was thankful though. I don't know what I would do if I saw him that night. I was beyond a rational state of mind and incredibly emotional. The reflecting I've been doing over the past two days doesn't help either.

How can the man that is supposed to protect me from everything, hit me? I don't even want to say that I'm hurt because I am so much more than that. Friday was a milestone, a bad one.

I wanted to do something that would upset my father. I can only think of one thing that he's ever truly cared about: Money.

I turn off the shower, walking straight to my computer. My mind was on autopilot as I sat in my desk chair in only a towel. Scrolling through thousands of clothes options: Evening gowns, prom dresses, ripped jeans, designer heels. You name it, I bought it. Purposely choosing to send a receipt by email. I wanted him to know. While shopping I came across body jewelry. The anger in my chest flickered. An even better idea popped up as I pull out my phone.

Athena's name is the one I clicked, I pulled up messages:

Know anywhere to get a good piercing?

<3

"What made you want a piercing?" Blaze laughs from the driver's seat; Athena next to her. I sat in the back. When I texted Athena that I wanted a piercing, Blaze was already with her. Turns out that they were skipping school as well.

They didn't ask why I didn't go to school, which I appreciated.

"Just in the mood for something spontaneous," I answer nonchalantly.

The only piercing I have is the first holes on my ears and that was done when I was a baby. Not only did I want a piercing, but I wanted one that my father could see and one that my father couldn't see.

Athena lets out a loud laugh, "I like that energy, you know I'm always down,"

"This guy did my spetum piercings," Blaze comments pulling up to a brick building. "He good at what he does and doesn't ask questions." She winks at me from the rearview mirror.

I didn't know much about these girls, but one thing I did know is that none of us were of age to be getting body piercings. As we walk through the parlor doors, the girls were greeted by a burly man. He was covered head to toe with tattoos. He had one of the largest gages I'd ever seen. Yet, he also had the brightest smile. I'm getting gentle giant vibes from him.

"Lincoln!" Blaze gives the large man a side hug, Athena shooting him a wave. "We have a new customer for you, she wants a piercing."

Lincoln glances at me, his smile doesn't falter causing mine to rise. He brings me straight into a hug with a laugh.

"What were you thinking, kid?" He pulls away.

"I want that bar that goes through the upper ear," I gesture to that part of my ear. "And then I saw this piercing in the middle of the ear-"

He hums walking behind the counter, "I think you mean an Industrial and Darth piercing."

He flips through a few pages showing me. We discuss what would be best for my ears, what shapes I wanted. The girls also decided to get a belly button ring. Of course, me being who I am, I decided that I would get that as well.

I hadn't thought about the pain all these piercing would be until Lincoln sat me in the chair. It still didn't click until he was cleaning the spots he would pierce. The girls thought that I should go first.

"Remember to breathe," Lincoln says while placing the gun to my ear.

Breathe, why would I forget to breat-

"Oh shit!" The actually piercing was a quick and sharp pinch. It was the after-effect that was getting me. The top of my ear was on fire. I didn't have to look at my ear, I know it's red.

"I like that one, I might get it myself." Athena was on my left, Blaze was somewhere flirting with the younger guy at the counter.

"Now, this one is going to hurt a little more than the next." Lincoln laughs silently.

Oh my goodness

I couldn't stop admiring the new additions to my body. The arrow and heart in my ear are suddenly my new obsession. My father has always said piercings are tacky. He's stated multiple times that I am to never add anything to my body while under his roof. Which I understand, his house, his rules. However, at this point, fuck him and his rules.

"There's a fight going on tonight, you down?" Blaze looked at me from the rearview mirror.

"Why not?" I shrug, immediately regretting it because it made the metal in my belly button aware of itself. That piercing looked pretty, but hurt like a bitch.

I was having fun, again. I was just living, excited. My ears were hot and I had an itch to start some shit. Another thought crept into my mind.

I wanted to see Axel

I inwardly groan at myself. Trying to forget about him was an unfortunately long process. Why can't I just skip to the part where I can walk by and him and pretend I don't know him?

I look towards the window now, drowning in the sound of conversation and music. Time seemed to fly in the parlor. We went in around lunchtime and got out around eight. All different types of people came in and out of the shop. A couple went and got their name tatted on each other.

Side eye

A man got a picture of his deceased mother on his back.

We even came across a war veteran that wanted all the names of his lost buddies on his forearm.

Whatever the case may have been all of these people had stories to share. The parlor was now my favorite place, whether I ever went there again or not.

"Listen, there's a lot of men here," Athena comments getting out of the car in front of what looks like an abandoned library. I furrow my brows but nod nonetheless.

Both girls walked through the building:

Silence

They laughed and told stories about this one fighter as they walked down dark halls. He apparently never lost. I tried to hold back my snort. I'm sure that was a bit of an exaggeration. The girls went downstairs, opening a door. That is when I heard all the noise. The loud yelling, the sound of skin-to-skin contact. The Oh's and Ah's could be heard around the ring. The lights were dim, yet the energy was high.

I found a clear spot that was a good distance from the match. The fight was almost over, but I was intrigued. The movements of both fighters, the heavy breathes, the cheering of the crowd.

I loved it

Then with one blow, the match was done. A fighter on the ground and another one standing proudly over him. Grey eyes searching the crowd. My heart stopped.

I no longer could hear anything, his eyes didn't meet mine, but they didn't need to. I could recognize those eyes anywhere. They were empty though, no emotion showed through them. At least none that I could decipher.

The second thing I noticed was the bruise on his face. It looked pretty gnarly. I itched to ask if he was okay, to ask if he needed anything. I silently cursed myself, he doesn't want to see me. I was a complete bitch last time we talked and he wasn't a saint himself.

I hadn't even registered that I was following him. I'd stopped at what I can assume his dressing room of sorts. The door was wide open, tempting me to just walk in. My voice was caught in my throat as I raced in my mind what to say to him.

All lies left my brain as I made eye contact with grey eyes in the mirror.

"Does it hurt?"

***

< Piercing that is described >

~ Chapter 11 ~

- -

He just looked at me

The realization that I was talking about his face hits him and turns his eyes briefly to his bruise. In all honesty, it didn't look bad. Compared to the other guy, Axel got the longer end of the stick.

I step further into the room, closing the door. The tension in the room is suffocating. His eyes seemed to be the only thing to keep my focus. I feel light-headed, the room on the verge of spinning. How can someone's eyes make your head reel?

"That was a cheap shot," I comment, taking a cold rag that laid on the counter and placing it on his cheek. I wonder if he can feel my hands shaking from behind the cloth.

I'm just praying to God he finds something else to stare at

"Who brought you here?"

I ignore his question, "How long have you been fighting?"

From the corner of my eye and can see him roll his. "Victoria, I asked you a quest-"

"I'm sorry," I blurt out, "You were just trying to help and I was a complete bitch."

Words that I've been wanting to say to him just fall out. I've practiced saying it in the mirror, in the shower. I think I even had a dream about saying it. Nonetheless, no matter how much I practiced, this is not the way I had imagined it. Not while he was silent and tired. Not while I was dapping a cold and probably dirty cloth on his face.

Yet, it still felt good to say

I was in the wrong, I can admit it. He didn't have to comfort me in the park, yet he did. Then I completely pushed him away.

"I know, baby, I know." He stands up, wrapping his arms around me.

"I didn't mean to be rude, I'm sorry if I hurt your feelings," I whisper from where my head was placed at the base of his shoulder. He chuckles slightly. I guess the apology was a little juvenile, but it was true. I could tell he was slightly hurt by my rude demeanor. Whether he wanted to admit it or not.

"It's alright, princess," He chuckles, releasing me from the hug.

Much to my dismay

"But you didn't answer my questions. Who brought you?" Axel collects his duffle bag and guides me out of the room. The hallways are dark, with busted lights. It smells strongly of cigarette smoke the further we go into the unfamiliar hallway.

"Blaze and Athena, but I lost them right before the fight," I answer. Axel nods at the passing men, they nod back. Why does everyone look so scary?

"I'll text them that I'll bring you home," He pulls out his phone, still walking swiftly through these neverending hallways.

The thought perked in my head of denying the ride. Saying that I was fully capable of catching a ride with the girls. That's what my ego wanted. However, I wanted nothing more but to spend one more bike ride with him. So I just kept quiet.

"So, that's what you did why skipping school today," Axel slyly comments as the cool fresh air hits our faces. We're finally out of the stuffy hallway. I didn't have to look at him to know he was gesturing to my new piercings. They were screaming for attention under the crisp blow of the wind.

"Call it an act of rebellion,"

"It looks good on you, did it hurt?" He mocks the words I said earlier.

I smile softly.

We're back

<3

I stand in front of my home, sighing. I could sneak into my room again, but my feet hurt. I was no longer in a spiteful mood. I was actually in a good one and dreading the next few moments that would lead to that being destroyed.

I go ahead and walk towards the kitchen, knowing my father was already there waiting for me. I was correct, he was there as well as a woman. This woman was not the campaign manager. I'd question it if I cared.

But I don't

"You didn't go to school today,"

"I did not,"

"You ran up two thousand dollars on my credit card,"

I don't think it was two thousand dollars.

"Keep up this bitchy attitude," He spits, his scorning eyes are the brightest light in the room. "I would send you away if I thought the public wouldn't notice. I would be bad on me, negative attention,"

"Doesn't it already look bad on you?" I retort right back.

"I hope you know as soon as you turn eighteen you're leaving this house. I don't want to hear or to speak to you again. Do you understand me? I don't know how the hell I got such an ungrateful daughter,"

"Look around Victoria! Look where you live! Everything I do for you, everything I give you. You need a real ass whooping and I've got half a mind to give it to you." The woman on his arms smooths the wrinkles out of his button. A wanton gaze thrown to his side - it makes me want to throw up.

"I've worked hard all my life and to get this," He gestures to me, "I must've killed someone in my past life."

"Emancipate me then," I simply shrug, " I'll be out of your hair,"

"Emancipation is a public record, people would ask questions,"

I groan, "Looks like people don't ask enough questions,"

I take myself to my room, ignoring whatever my father was still complaining about. I am so beyond tired of all this shit. He complains about me every day, yet won't do anything about it. This situation will so much easier if just ignored me.

He never takes any action. He's full of empty promises. He's been threatening to send me away for years. Even when I was a little girl; I would ugly crying, on my knees, pleading forgiveness from my father. His gaze was always cold and his mouth always hurled hurtful words.

Eventually, I just stopped crying. I stopped listening. After a while, it seemed like he would be angry either way.

It's that he goes out of his way to insult me. I guess my father is proof that when you have a child love isn't guaranteed. The rational part of me knows that this isn't was he truly feels. That something deeper is going on. The other side of me doesn't care, I know I shouldn't be treated like this. This can't possibly be how other kids are treated.

Love

I start to hate that word more and more every day

I hate thinking. I hate having to hold this in, but I have no one to tell it to. The only thing I can vent to is my mirror. I like to think of myself as a strong person, but sometimes, just sometimes:

I just need someone to hug me and tell me that I'm not as much as a nuisance as I feel at times

I jump at the sound of a clink on my window. My back against my door and I have my knees to my chest, bawling my eyes out. I roughly wipe my face and walk to the window.

It was very dark outside, I barely saw it:

A raven

Black eyes looking back at me. Maybe it was because I'm said and delusion, but I could've sworn the same raven from my french class. I scoff a small laugh.

A bird is the most loyal thing in my life right now

~ Chapter 12 ~

S chool has a certain smell

Not necessarily a bad or pungent smell, but a smell nonetheless. Once it enters your nose you immediately recognize it. Something that says:

Oh yeah, I'm in school

When I was in elementary school, I liked school. I liked to learn new things and play with friends. Times, when homework was fun and reading was for enjoyment. Even now I don't hate school. The older I've gotten the more I just feel - indifferent - about school.

It's the smell of the metal lockers, it's the smell of stinky students, it's the smell of over perfumed girls, it's the smell of shit-talking teachers. All of these smells mixed together with the occasional tears.

Makes the smell of the school

"Vic!" A voice calls out from behind me.

I turn to see Olivia's blonde hair bouncing down the hallway towards my direction, "Yeah?"

"Okay so since you missed yesterday, I'll catch you up with everything. We have a pep rally today, it'll cut through your first and second block-"

I'm always down for something to get me out of French

"Pep rally? For what?" We change course and make our way to the gym.

Pep rally schedule depended on your lunch and your lunch depends on your grade. They really don't have to separate us like that though. I'm sure every student could fit in the gym for one pep rally if we really wanted to.

"Nothing, in particular, just to raise spirits and school pride I guess."

Olivia and I had a good conversation about nothing important. It was moments like these that reminded me of how our friendship used to be. Our good times were good but our bad times were toxic. I love Olivia- when she's not being a bitch.

"What the hell is that?"

Olivia gasps as we enter the gym. I have to bite back a snicker. Standing on the gym floor was some kind of large box filled with water.

"It's a dunking both," I snort, "The real question is why is it in the gym?"

"Find a seat ladies and gentlemen, we have a wonderful surprise for you!" Ms. Jenni, our assistant principal sings into the microphone.

A few mutual friends get Olivia and I's attention. They gesture to the seats they saved for us at the top of the bleachers and we head our way to their area.

"Who do you think is going to be getting dunked?" A red-head quirks as we take our seats. I'd seen her before and I'm pretty sure I've had a small conversation with her, but I did not know her name.

"I hope to the heavens it's Ms. Boucher,"

I chuckle at the comment. It would truly be a lovely sight for Ms. Boucher to be dunked. She would never let that happen though, I'm positive she was the one that thought up this idea.

"Quiet down." Ms. Boucher pops out of nowhere with the microphone.

Speak of the devil and he shall appear

"We know it's halfway through the year, school is getting boring, so we wanted to surprise our wonderful students!" Mrs. Jenni brightens again, "We're going to take a poll. You have three choices: Mr. Knight, Ms. Boucher, and Myself!"

"Did I hear that right?" I ask out loud, "I know she did not just say Ms. Boucher, oh she's going to have a whole fit,"

"Even worst, Ms. Boucher is crazier than we thought if she thinks this whole student body isn't going to vote for her."

I like this girl, I need to find out her name

"Raise of hands for Mr. Knight-" Mrs. Jenni raises a hand over Mr. Knight's head. Out of all of the two hundred students in this gym currently. I'd say about five rose their hands.

Mr. Knight was an administer. I haven't really had too many run-ins with him as well as I haven't really heard anyone complain about him. Mrs. Jenni moves on to raise her hand over herself.

She knows what's about to happen, that's why she waited to judge Ms. Boucher last

I didn't see any hands raised for Mrs. Jenni, but at that same time, I really wasn't looking that hard. I was just preparing to start recording when Ms. Boucher got dunked. Mrs. Jenni moves on, hesitantly. Raising her hand and taking a deep breath.

"Ms. Bouche-"

She didn't even get to finished the cheers and hands in the crowd cut her off. I didn't raise my hand, I didn't have to. It was without a doubt Ms. Boucher who was chosen to go into the dunking booth. What I was more captivated by was Ms. Boucher's face. Utter shock rested on her hard features. Her face was red, whether it was from embarrassment or anger, I was not sure. I would feel bad for her, but she just gave me a forty-five on our last quiz.

So in the booth, you go... bitch

"This was rigged!" The red-faced woman shouts from the gym floor, her actions remind me slightly of an infuriated toddler. The stomping of the foot and the wave of the hands all add up.

"I work hard every day to teach for this school and this is what I get!" Ms. Boucher was giving everybody a piece of her mind. We were gonna listen to her today. "I refuse to be belittled and insulted in my own place of work!"

With that, she stomps out.

My mouth? Dropped.

My eyes? Wide.

Hotel? Trivago.

"If you'll stay in your seats, we'll be right back." Mrs. Jenni musters up a smile a scoots in the directions Ms. Boucher left to. I look at Olivia.

"Fuck that."

"Please, tell me someone got that on video!" I laugh walking outside.

We decided since the failed pep rally freed up a whole block. We would just hang outside of the cafeteria.

"Bitch-" The redhead draws out, "I got you, here, give me your number."

I hand her my phone:

Scarlette is her name

Huh, fitting

The girls laugh about the event earlier as I let my mind wander. Ms. Boucher was truly the character. I'd never know a woman so mean could be so sensitive. She was out of her mind if she thought the student body hasn't been waiting for a chance to get back at this woman. Hell! The teachers too. I bet my librarian friend is laughing her ass off.

Dark hair and a leather jacket distract me. The figure walked swiftly around the brick corner of the school.

"I'll be back, I have to use the bathroom-" I lie, walking towards where I'd just seen the figure.

When I turned the corner, no one was there. The side of the school was completely bare except for the two dumpsters. I start to turn around when I'm pushed against the brick wall gently.

"Looking for someone, doll?"

Chapter 13

"Jesus Christ, don't do that!"

I shoot a look at Axel, his stupid face covered in that sly smirk of his. The mind of a teenage boy is truly juvenile. What could he even be doing back here anyway?

"Sorry, sweetheart, didn't mean to scare you." He leans against the brick wall, pulling out a cigarette and lighting it. He really doesn't live down the bad boy status.

"Were you at the pep rally?" I smile, he takes note of my excitement and chuckles slightly.

"No, but I heard about it," He removes the cigarette from his lips, blowing away from my face, "That lady is a bitch though,"

I scoff, "Tell me about it,"

"What are you doing out of area?" He leans in closer to where I stood, "Weren't you told to stay in the gym?"

"Doesn't that sign say no smoking?" I gesture to the white and red sign right above his head.

"Touché."

He throws the burning cigarette on the ground. Stomping it into the gravel with his leather boot. It was such a simple gesture, so... normal.

But when he did it, it was inexplicably attractive. In fact, I take this time to check out what he was wearing. White t-shirt and dark wash jeans. Checking him out was completely unnecessary, I didn't even have to look at him to know he looked good. Part of me thinks that's what keeps me from ever actually being irritated at him.

His eyes drift from mine to something behind me. The small smile that he managed to let slip past his lips quickly went away. He grabs my upper arm, pinning me to the wall, his body in front of me. Before I could manage a few colorful words, his lips were on my ear.

"Your boyfriend is staring at us,"

Boyfriend? Oh?

"What are you talking about?" I try and peek around him, yet his large frame against mine was actively stopping me from doing that.

He shifts himself to the side. Still holding my arm gently, but his shoulder was now leaning on the brick wall. I quickly took note of how the sun shown in his grey eyes, if I didn't care about embarrassing myself, I'd stare into them. They were simply enchanting.

Looking to where Axel used to stand, I only see Lucas Saunters. That couldn't possibly be who he was talking about.

"Saunters?" I turn my head slightly to catch Axel nod his.

Lucas Saunters

He was in my french class. I'd never had a solid conversation with him, but we were aware of each other's presence. We'd gone to middle school together. He has been the quarterback of the football team since I can remember. I'd never really noticed him, or given him a second glance. My fullest extent of interest in him was when my friend had a crush on him in ninth grade.

"I've never even talked to that boy," I look back at Axel fully.

It was true, Lucas was definitely staring. It was the reason that I didn't know. Lucas was sitting on the tables tops of the seating area outside. Jock friends all around him, yet he was staring at me.

More specifically Axel's hand on my arm

"What do you think he wants?" I subconsciously move closer to Axel, uncomfortable under Luca's gaze.

"You."

<3

I sigh, unlocking the door to my house. They, unfortunately, never did finish the pep rally. They told all kids to just resume their classes on a modified schedule and never brought up the dunking booth again.

I think earlier to Axel's last words to me before he got a call. I didn't think Lucas wanted me. I'm afraid I'm not really his type. I don't actually know his type, but I know it's not me. Maybe he wants the homework? That would be unfortunate because I have not done it.

There wasn't much different about him, he looked like every other aver-agely attractive guy. I'd managed to bring him up in a conversation with Olivia. She says he's 'God's true gift to Earth', but again that is a very large exaggeration.

"Victoria," My father's voice rings familiar as I enter the kitchen. I immediately hold my breath, preparing myself for whatever he had to let me know. I can firmly say that I have not done anything to anger him today.

"I need to talk to you."

I nod.

"As you know, your mother and I have had some problems. The divorce was good for both of us," He stirs the drink in his cup: Whiskey. I could smell it from where I stood. "You know Carol?"

It was a statement, yet I didn't actually know who Carol was. I furrow my brows, hearing heels click from the foyer. My father's campaign manager walks in with a shit-eating grin. She kisses him on the forehead, before turning her gaze to me.

Honey, he was just with another woman-

"I've found happiness with her, make sure you're free February fourteenth. That's when we'll make the wedding announcement."

My heart dropped

"...wedding?" My voice comes out hoarse, shocked.

I really didn't want to start with him, I knew whatever I was about to say would not affect him in any way. I just couldn't let this go. It hadn't even been a week since he kicked my mother out. Now he was marrying his mistress?

"It's been days,"

"Do. Not. Start." He clenches his jaw, that whore of his latching onto his arm. In some poor attempt to calm him.

Sorry, darling, that only works with people that actually love each other

"When does it end? When will you stop?"

"I have no idea what you're referring to, but listen to me closely." He sets his glass down, "This disobedience I've been getting from you recently will stop. Do you hear me? If your grandfather was still alive he was would be ashamed of the way I've let you talk to me"

I have been reckless, I will make a note to stop speaking.

"You need a motherly figure and your mother is in no space to be that for you,"

Note = Broken

"I've said it before and I'll say it again: She will never be my mother. I will play by your rules. I will stop talking back to you. I will move out on my eighteenth birthday. I will try to be the perfect daughter that you want the public see," I seethe through my teeth, "But I will not pretend that your whore is my mother,"

"I'll try and make you look like a perfect father, but as soon as the cameras turn off, do not forget that you are the farthest thing from it," I must've looked crazy standing in my classic kitchen with the wildest expression on my face. I feel like my father only says things like this to get a rise out of me, there's no way he thinks talking like this is okay.

"You will do as I say!" He stood up, towering over me from where he stood behind the island.

But that's okay because I was ready for him to hit me today. If he were going to hit me, he better knock me the fuck out. I was not with his shit today. I felt my blood hot in my veins, I was ready for anything. Anything he wanted to say, he better say it now.

"I'm not going to repeat myself,"

I should've felt a sting on my face right there, but, I didn't.

"I never wanted this life!" My father roars, the woman at his arm backs up completely,

"I never wanted you!"

~ Chapter 14 ~

"**W**as that supposed to hurt my feelings?"

It did

"You have not earned the right to call yourself my father. Now I told you what I was going to do. I will respect you because I am under your roof. I'll help you get into the office, but I will not treat you as if we are family outside of the public eye," I start up the stairs, before pausing to turn and look at him again, "Your words don't hurt me anymore."

It's always something with him. I'm always coming home to some sort of arrangement or lecture. I mean, he must get tired of yelling at me.

Doesn't he just want to ignore me?

What does he get out of yelling at me?

I slam my bedroom door, it seems like I do that a lot. My hard outer exterior did well to not show my burning heart.

How could my father say that to me? It's not like I didn't already know he didn't want me, but when it comes out of his mouth, it just hurts differently. My eyes burn, but not with tears. I didn't feel like crying. I didn't feel anything but hot.

I could cry later, but right now I needed to find a job

<3

I've been job hunting for hours. I originally started out on my computer; texting Athena if she knew of any jobs. I then slowly moved to riding around downtown looking for 'help wanted' signs. I found a few, but the small bookworm in me was begging to become a waitress at a small diner in a small town.

I needed money. I would live under my father's roof until it becomes legal for me to move out. Even if he offered me a moving out fund. I wouldn't take it. Once I turned eighteen I wanted nothing to do with him.

With that being said, cutting contact off with a parent isn't ideal. However, it's clear to me that he would never be the father that I needed. Whatever demons he was dealing with at the moment, obviously have temporarily won.

The ring of my phone takes my attention away from the passing buildings. I quickly pick it up, returning my eyes to the road.

"Yes?"

"Girl, what in the hell do you want a job for?"

I chuckle lightly, "I need money, hun,"

"Well, I wouldn't let you work where I work. That wouldn't be appropriate, but I think I could hook you up with something,"

"Wouldn't be appropriate? What are you? A Stripper?" I snort, pulling over to the side of the road.

She pauses.

"Oh shit, I didn-"

"Just kidding," Her laugh rings in my phone's speaker, "Even though that is the end goal eventually."

Love that energy

"Come meet me at Sleepy Hollow Drive, the fork in the road,"

"Okay." I hang up, hitting a U-turn.

Sleepy Hollow Drive was a rather long road, but I knew what fork she was talking about. I look at my outfit. It wasn't bummy, but I would've worn something a little more professional to meet a potential employer.

I can't help but let my mind drift to my mother. It had been two weeks, maybe? From the last time, I saw her. I didn't have a way to contact her and she certainly didn't try to get into contact with me. I, again, was not upset at her. It's useless being mad at a woman that can't even remember her own name, let alone call her daughter.

I wasn't mad at anyone, not now, not when I know what I have to do.

I drive down Sleepy Hallow. It's always been a pretty road. It's in the middle of a few pastures. Then the fork in the road turns into trees. I had an idea about what building Athena was talking about. There weren't too many buildings out here.

I could point out Athena's eyes from anywhere. They glowed brightly under the golden hour of sunlight. She was standing outside the building in question, waving at me. I was correct in my assumption earlier. I did know the place.

It was the gym, I saw Axel fight a few nights ago. I park and hop out of my car, giving Athena a tight hug.

"Thanks for coming through!" I smile, pushing my wild hair out of my face.

"Of course, don't even mention it," She waves me off with a smile, walking me through the front of the gym.

Even though I didn't see much of the gym when it was packed and almost completely dark. I could tell this wasn't the room the fight took place in. This was more of the training section. Lots of punching bags and treadmills. There was a large ring in the middle of the room but unlike the one from the real fight. This one didn't have a cage on it.

"Daddy!" Athena yells at the top of her lungs, even with few guys in the gym at the moment all of them just continue doing what they do. Like it was a common occurrence.

I'm sure it was

A tanned, dark-haired man stalks out of one of the doors upstairs. A wide smile on his face, and the same piercing green eyes as Athena.

"Sì, Tesoro?" The large man sings.(Yes, Treasure)

"Il mio amico ha bisogno di un lavoro e stai assumendo papà." The unknown language flows fluently out of her mouth. (My friend needs a job and you're hiring, papa.)

"Eight an hour, three times a week. She'll clean the gym and tend to the members," He's referring to me now.

"Sounds great, sir-" Is all I manage to get out.

He was hundreds of feet away from me and on a totally different level, but his dominance still gushed out throughout the entire gym. He was scary.

"That's it? I have the job?" I turn to Athena with a smile.

"Yup, that's all it takes. My father has been complaining about the gym stinking and being a mess for weeks now. When you texted me earlier I figure this was perfect to kill two birds with one stone," She smiles, "Now, let me settle something in the back and I'll be right out to explain the job to you."

I nod, setting my stuff down. Although this wasn't exactly the small-town diner that I was hoping for. I could see a few perks of working here. Maybe I could get a six-pack before summer started.

Or watch other people get six-packs

The small sound of a flutter attracts my attention to the large window behind me. In the middle flew a pretty little raven. Eyes dark, but warm. I smiled, even if the pretty bird couldn't register it.

"Victoria?"

I turn my head, "Kaiden, right?"

I walk towards the red benches. The whole bad boy crew seemed to be gathered there. Well, everyone except for Axel.

"Yeah, what are you doing here?"

"Umm," I trial off looking around. I really didn't want to tell him that I was getting a job here. He, of course, would eventually find out. "I'm here with Athena."

That wasn't a complete lie, I was here with Athena. Kaiden nods anyway, a smile returns to his face as he welcomes me over to where they were sitting.

I wanted to ask where Axel was, but I knew what that would look like so I refrain.

"Do you guys have another fight? Or do you just work out here?"

"Aw, did you miss me, beautiful?" Heavy, sweaty arms drape on my shoulders with a familiar deep voice.

"First of all," I remove his arms from my shoulders, "You're sweaty and not to break your heart, but I'm here with Athena" I fix my jean jacket that he managed to ruffle with his heavy, stinky arms.

"You've already broken my heart, baby, this doesn't phase me," His prominent smirk irks the shit out of me.

Where did he even come from?

"Oh my God, shut up." I roll my eyes, "I think Athena called me, I have to go, but I'll talk to you gentlemen later," I smile at the rest of the boys.

Athena clearly didn't call me

Before I could turn all the way around, Axel's large hand grabs at the top of my arm.

"I'll talk to you later, princess."

✳✳✳

< Outfit that's described >

~ Chapter 15 ~

"No, the edges are rigid."

Olivia comments taking the smooth rock out of my hand and writing down on our lab sheet. I roll my eyes. We were doing a small lab for Marine Biology, seeing how saltwater affects erosion on rocks and other objects in the sea.

"I have to go to the bathroom." I tried not to let her hear the irritation in my voice. I notified the teacher before walking out of the lab.

I just took a deep breath. I can be quick-tempered when provoked and I could feel the words that I've been suppressing for a while, trying to come up. I taste the hurtful words on the back of my tongue but I refused to let them hit the air. My temper is the same as my father's. Just one of the things that I hated about myself. It was a gift in some situations, but a demon in almost all of them.

I strolled down the hall, keeping a close eye on the time. I was planning to be gone for ten minutes. I'll cool off and return to the lab with Olivia.

A large warm force is was reminds me that I'm in a hallway. The person's chest really did a number on my lungs. I stood panting, looking for the idiot that walked right into me.

"Sorry," I mumble despite it not being my fault, "My fault."

No, it wasn't

"No, no-" The boy speaks, "My bad, I shouldn't walk and text."

Damn, right

I look up at the boy, my brains take a second to recognize his face. I blame it on the lack of oxygen. The person who bumped into me was the one and only:

Lucas Saunters

"Victoria? Right?" He gestures to me with a friendly half-smile. I nod.

"Congratulations on your father."

I frown, confused about what he meant. He notices, speaking again.

"The wedding," He elaborates, "My dad got the invite a few days ago. I meant to congratulate you earlier, but I guess I couldn't find the chance." His smile never falters.

I had to catch myself, I almost let out a scoff at my father's new martial plans. I remember my place.

"Oh!" I feign surprise, "Of course, I'm happy that my parents have come to an agreement that works best for them. I actually really like my dad's fiance."

Perfect daughter mode: On.

"I'll see you on the fourteenth." He winks.

"You'll be there? I'm sorry, I just didn't know your family had any relation with my father." My father has never spoken of the Saunters, but then again, I don't really talk to my father.

"Not a lot," He answers, "They worked together before your dad decided to run for Mayor."

I nod, shooting him a soft smile. "You'll have to save me a dance."

I start to make my way back to the lab, seeing as this conversation with Lucas has taken up my ten minutes.

"Definitely." He comments behind me.

<3

"We should hang out together for Valentine's day," Mia suggests as she meets us outside. It was the end of the day and we just talking outside.

I sigh, "I can't, my dad is getting married."

"Your parents are getting married again? What, like renewing their vows?" I adore Mia for asking that question.

"No my parents have been divorced for a while." I lie.

"Oh, shit. My bad, I didn't know."

"You're all good." I wave her off. I just appreciate that she asked.

"That's one of my fears." She comments, I chuckle softly.

"What? Your parents getting a divorce?" She nods, I glance at her thoughtfully. "My parents are better separate."

"It's not a big deal-" Olivia cuts into the conversation, biting into her apple. "It might be even better than them being married. I mean, come on, two Christmases."

I shrug, not wanting to start anything with her. I had a small headache and I really just wanted to go home. The only reason why I wasn't walking to my car right now was that I didn't want to be rude. I haven't talked to these girls in a while, even though my feelings towards them have started to change I'm not sure I want to burn bridges. That's not a good idea in high school.

My eyes caught on a group of people standing across the walkway in the student parking lot. They were laughing, not caring about anything. They were having fun. Grey eyes caught onto mine. Immediately the only thing I wanted to do was walk over to them. I wanted to talk to them.

I could help the small smile that played on my lips as I watch the boy monkey around. Axel didn't mouth anything but his stare was welcoming. I could see the colors play in his eyes, he could see I wanted to be over there, yet I wasn't moving. He was curious.

"Who are you looking at-" Olivia asks, turning around. The girls follow her gaze.

"Axel?" She looks at me, "I was just kidding when I was talking about the whole hot thing. They're bad news. He might kill you just for looking at him." She laughs.

Normally I would just brush off that comment. I don't know why I was sensitive to the topic today. This school day for some reason has been a very bad day for us. I couldn't find any common ground with her.

"What? Have you ever even had a conversation with him?" I frown.

She scoffs, "People talk, and rumors don't appear out of thin air,"

"They literally do- like literally,"

"Why are you getting so defensive?" She pauses, a smirk falling to her lips, "Oh, you think he's cute. Vic's got a little crush,"

"I don't see why standing up for him means that I have a crus-"

"You should drop it, it's not going to go anywhere. He's probably a player,"

"Prime - fucking - example! Where have you heard that? You just pulled that out of your ass!" I exasperate.

"Oh please, you can tell, look at him-"

"That's fitting, isn't? Coming from you."

"And what the hell is that suppose to mean?" I see her green eyes perk, this is the fight she's been picking at since she woke up. She wanted an argument and I hadn't been giving it to her. I still wasn't. I didn't care enough to argue with her.

"Ponder it."

I walk off towards Axel, now noticing his eyes haven't moved from me. I wonder if he heard what she said about him?

"Hi." I smile softly as I get close enough to them. The smiles they automatically shoot to me make my heart warm. My small argument with Olivia quickly pushed to the back of my mind.

"Hey! Did you get the video I sent to you?" Scarlette asks from my right. I hadn't even noticed she was standing in the group. It makes sense though.

Good energy seems to vibe together

"Oh my gosh, yes!" I recall the video of the pep rally.

"What's up bitch?" Athena greets me with a hug.

After all the hugs and greets, I ended up next to Axel. His arm resting heavily on my shoulder. I didn't say anything, in too much of a good mood to even comment on it. They continue about a conversation on the fight that was supposed to take place tomorrow night. Only this time it was Kaiden fighting and not Axel.

I happened to be working tomorrow so I'll be there anyway.

"Loverboy's staring again," Axel whispers in my ear. I frown up at him, looking around to find out what he's talking about.

Sure enough,

Lucas Saunters was staring... again

<h1 align="center">~ Chapter 16 ~</h1>

I'm trying to pick out my dress

My father and I have recently only been communicating through text. He would give me instructions and I would read them. I'd only respond when I had a question. I liked it better this way. My father was... tolerable.

Their wedding announcement - dinner - gala thing was coming up. My father has instructed me to wear red, as he and his mistress would. It was Valentine-themed, so the people that were attending were supposed to wear: Gold, white, and black.

At least that's what the invitation expressed

With the little shopping spree I went on with my dad's card, fortunately, I ordered a red gown that I thought was pretty. It was modest, elegant. My father might have a small problem with the tightness of the dress and the slit, but he has a problem with everything.

My phone's alarm goes off.

Today I started my first day at work. It was eleven at night. My boss needed me to clean up before the big match. This was the one Kaiden was fighting in, all day I had been talking to him. I wanted to make sure he was okay.

I couldn't lie, the underground fighting ring intrigued me. I would totally start fighting if I could bear the thought of someone punching me in the face. Another part of me is interested because of my father's hatred towards it. As much as I try to convince myself that I'm not resentful, I am.

I try not to be, I really do

When I see other kids happy with their parents the mean green monster rears his ugly face in the back of my head. I wasn't just upset at my father though. I have two parents. Both have wronged me.

I put on a quick little outfit and I snuck through my bedroom window. My father had installed motion cameras in the front yard. He says it's for protection, but I know it's because he wants to keep tabs on me. I still hadn't forgotten what he mentioned a while ago.

He's had someone following me, but shit

Let them follow

It's not going to change anything

As long as I don't cause a scene, I won't push my father past his limits. He cares what the public sees. So I'll make sure that the public only sees a perfect family unit.

I unlock my car, getting in. I planned on taking the long way to work. I wanted time to think everything out. I often have to do this.

Think it out

I have to get in my car and drive. Right now, I was perfecting the speech that was to be made at the wedding announcement. The whole thing was going to be a lie and it had to sound good. I needed to be emotional. I needed to be happy for the couple. This was going to be the hardest part of the night.

I don't want to think about that anymore, I want to think of something happier.

Axel immediately comes to mind, I let it. He was going to be there tonight, there was no doubt. Maybe part of me put on the tight black leggings because I knew, of course, that was just a small thought. The main reason I wore this outfit to work, was because I knew I needed to let my new piercing breathe if I was going to be working.

The gym comes up in view, I let out a content sigh while getting out of my car. The only bad part of this job was the late hours on school nights. I would be tired in the morning, but I wouldn't be broke.

"What's up bitch?" Athena greets me with a hug as I walk through the door. I smile widely, returning the hug.

"It's kind of empty for fight night," I state as I walk to the back.

"The gym is closed for everyone except fighters, they just went into their changing rooms a few minutes before you arrived. Their warmups are done and Kaiden will probably come out and hang in VIP. The other guy will stay in his changing room." She explains as I get out everything I need to clean. After the tour she gave me on the first day, I am aware of what the gym needs for prep.

"I assume to prevent fighting?" She nods.

"Once you're done come on over to VIP, everybody is already there?" She smiles and makes her way to an upstairs area.

I get to mopping the ring first. Dry blood and sweat covered the red flooring. The smell was absolutely putrid. Many people had been pinned against this same flooring.

Can they not smell it? This is another reason why I couldn't fight.

As I start to scrub the floor, the bright red color of the mat starts to pop out. Turns out that under the sweat and dirt, is a nice red and white color mat. I didn't even know the mat was lined white before I took a mop to it.

I hop out, satisfied with the final look of the ring. Next, I would place the wrappings in their changing room.

These boys didn't wear boxing gloves, but they did wrap their hands with some hand wrap. Kaiden's was black and the other boy's, whose name I did not know, was blue. I dropped Kaiden's off no problem, but I was scared to enter the other boy's room.

"I would have said hi earlier, but watching you clean the mat was too good to disrupt." The voice sends a small shiver down my spine, "Good evening, angel, how are you feeling?"

"You know that's just weird?" I laugh continuing down the hallway as he walks next to me.

"Why were you cleaning it anyway?" He chuckles to himself, leaning on the wall as I get in front of the other fighter's door.

"It was dirty and I need the money," I state simply, knocking on the door.

It didn't take long for the door to fly open. Behind where was once a wooden door, stands a tall blonde man. He had a neat beard and mean scowl. He wasn't scowling at me, it's just the way his face sits.

"Here is your wrap, you are to have these on before fighting in the ring," I try to sound like I know what I'm talking about. Seeing as I've totally forgotten the exact words I was supposed to say.

"Thanks, sweetie," He smirks, grabbing the wrap from me before giving me a once over. "Once I win you can take these wraps off of me,"

"Once you win?" I mock him, "That's cute."

I turn away from the door before he can grab and kill me. Axel looks at me amused. He would like it if that big man killed me. I bet it would make his day.

"Wipe that smirk off your face," I comment, starting my way to VIP.

"You're cute," He snorts.

"I know."

He falls into step next to me, amusement literally radiating off of him. It was slowly, but surely pissing me off.

What was so fucking funny?

"What do you need the money for?" He brings up our conversation before the door opened, "Your dad's running for Mayor,"

"My dad's running for Mayor, not me,"

"What? Daddy cut you off."

At this point, I was a few paces in front of him. His statement makes me spin around to meet him. He stops right before colliding chests with me. His breath lightly fanning my face. This was just a sign that maybe we were a little too close.

"Even after knowing me, you still think me and my father are one of the same?" I shake my head lightly.

That wasn't fair. Axel didn't know me. I didn't know Axel. The only difference is, I didn't hold Axel's past, whatever it may be, against him. Something tells me, when he goes home it's not to a perfect house either.

Well, of course, it's not

If it was, he wouldn't be here

"I didn't think you to be the judgy type," I pan around, continuing my walk.

"I'm not,"

"Could've fooled me."

<3

The fight had started. The VIP section had an amazing view to it. There was a scoreboard, I hadn't seen it the last fight.

Axel sat across from me in the booth. I noticed his small glances towards me, I chose to ignore them. He thinks I'm upset at him. He was wrong. I'm over our small argument in the hall if you could even call it that.

Right now, I was just enjoying the fight. Athena sat on the left of me explaining what was happening in my ear. She wasn't lying when she said everybody was here: Tyler, Noah, Blaze, Scarlette, and Axel. They were all here.

"I give the guy five minutes," Tyler comments, I look at him.

"Why? What's his weakness?"

"He has a bad knee and too much muscle," Noah answers my question.

I turn to look at the other fighter in the ring. He was stumbling slightly, and he was huge. At first glance, I probably wouldn't assume that he was hurt.

I hum. "Nice observation,"

"Thank you, Victoria." Tyler smiles boyishly at me, which I return.

BOOM

The sound of a body hitting the mat makes my head jerk to the ring. Sure enough, the large man was on the ground and out cold. The crowd under us cheered loudly as the ref held up Kaiden's hand.

"Do I have to get the wraps back?"

***

< Outfit that is mentioned >

~ Chapter 17 ~

"You think that's appropriate?"

That is the first thing my father has said to me in days. He was referring to the dress I put on for one of his press conferences. After the new year, my father's campaign has started to pick up. This is the time of year when we would start making public appearances.

The conference was a small one. It wasn't going to be detrimental by any means. Nevertheless, as my father says:

'All press is good press.'

"Sorry," I apologize simply.

I was not in a combative mood. I was sitting in the back of the limo trying desperately to suppress my opinions. I may or may not be asked any questions and all of the answers to those hypothetical questions needed to be short, sweet, and vague.

I took theatre in sixth grade, this was going to be a piece of cake.

This would be the last press conference before my father's wedding announcement on Valentine's day.

"They want you to get out of the left side of the car and then the purple carpet shall lead you to your rooms," The drive states the instructions as the car comes to a halt.

"Miss. Victoria, you should get out first."

I nod and mutter a small 'Okay' shifting myself in front of the door. Through the tinted windows, I could see the press talk amongst each other. Positioning their cameras to get the best shot. They all have a hungry look in their eyes, every last one of them. I don't hold that against them though.

Sometimes the greed for gossip can silence our sense of humanity

The door opens and I plaster a bright smile on my face. People behind the lines shoving microphones against guards and throwing out personal questions. I continue to wave and smile as I make my way down the carpet.

A short woman greets us at the door, her tone in a frenzy:

"You'll be on in twenty minutes!"

<3

"What is the main goal you want to achieve if you were to be elected Mayor?"

It's been a solid thirty minutes of my father answering the same questions just formatted differently. I want to say press conferences last an hour, but I honestly wouldn't know. Thirty minutes feel like a lifetime to me.

"As soon as I get into office," My father revs, "I promise to get rid of the whole underground scene. The drag racing and the fights have simply poisoned our youth for years and I refuse to let it go on any longer."

I swear I've heard him rehearse that line hundreds of times. At this point why do they even bother asking? It's literally the same answer every time they ask.

The reporter sits down as many others raise their hands to be picked next. My father calls on a pretty woman and the deep breath my future stepmother takes is only audible to people sitting at the table.

I bite my cheek.

"Your daughter goes to public school. How does it make you feel that she might come across one of the people associated with the drag racing?"

My heart picks up its beating pace and I cut my eyes to him.

"It scares me," He looks me directly in my eye, "My daughter is a strong young lady and I know she can withstand peer pressure, but it's the other children that I worry about. The ones that get easily sucked into these types of things."

To the press, it may have looked like he was praising me. I, however, knew better. He was mocking me because I have been to the underground scene. His condescending tone seemed to have gone unnoticed by the crowd.

My father reaches towards me and I involuntarily flinch. Which, again, had gone unnoticed by the crowd. My father's reach turns into a short hug and he recoils back to his seat. The expression on his face made my heart pick up once again.

"Miss Victoria!" A man waves his hand, "How are you feeling about your parent's divorce? I understand they've been married for sixteen years. That must've been hard for you." The man feigns concern as he shoves a recorder to my face.

I glance at my father before I speak up, "My parents, I know, will always love each other. With that being said, it's best if they were apart."

I regretted saying that, my answer seemed a little too formal - detached - even. Not something a sixteen-year-old should be able to conjure up.

"Very mature of you, Miss. Victoria,"

"Both my parents have gone out of their way to make sure I understand the divorce and why it was happening. I just want them both to be happy. They deserve it." I tried to do some damage control.

The crowd nods in admiration another reporter perks up.

"Mr. Beckette, your daughter seems so well mannered. What are some tips on controlling your children for the people at home?"

I bite my cheek again.

"Discipline is extremely important, actions have consequences."

You son of a bitch-

"I want the children to be safe, I love my family and I couldn't imagine a life without them. I will put my all into helping broken families if I get elected." My father turns to me, "No one should feel unloved."

The hardest thing I've ever had to do was keep my face solid as he mocked me in front of the press. Not ever in my life has he been so... mean. I want to be angry and I want to resent him. I can pretend I do all I want, but at the end of the day, the warm tears that burn at the back of my eyes remind me that I'm just heartbroken. I'm unloved and that's what makes me bitter.

I'm still the little girl from a broken home

Everything is temporary, but this pain - this scar - is not

I clench my jaw to get through the rest of the press conference. As soon as the press cleared out I made my way to the limo and continued to sit in silence. Not like it matter, the other two adults in the back of the limo didn't make a move to acknowledge me either. Neither did they talk to each other. The cutting glances my father's mistress shot at him tells me that there will be an argument tonight, probably about that female reporter.

The ding of my phone cuts through the silence in the car. I move to check it:

I left him on read, my face gets hot from embarrassment. Why couldn't he have just left it alone? What did he want me to say? He knows, so now what? Nothing.

That's why I didn't say anything in the first place, he would know too much information and I would still be stuck in my situation. Him knowing that small fact does absolutely nothing to change the current facts. I was still stuck.

I blink to clear my mind, knowing if I kept on the topic I would soon lose control.

I wouldn't cry

Not in this car

Not right now

Not anymore

***

< Outfit that is described >

Also, I wanted to comment on the cute little message thing I did! Look at it! I found a fake message creator and I thought it was so cool. I will do this when the messages are important to character development and the story. Other small text messages will stay in italics. Let me know how you feel about this because I don't mind removing it if it looks dumb.

Bye, Love you!

Author

~ Chapter 18 ~

"You can't even pretend to be a good daughter."

Is the last statement my father made towards me as I went straight to my room from the limo. I don't think he believes that. If he truly believed I did poorly at the meeting, he would've said something in the limo.

Maybe its the stress of office that he needs relieving from

If he acts like this during the campaign. I can only imagine what he'll act like if he gets the position Mayor. We'd have to live in completely different houses if I wanted to make it to my eighteenth birthday.

I wasn't focused on my father right now. I was focused on how I would move forward after the texts from Axel.

Nothing was going to change

Nothing could be done

I take a deep breath as my back hits my room door. I needed my head to be clear. I needed to straighten out my feelings. I throw open my balcony doors. I don't use this balcony very often because most of the time I didn't want to be seen. However, right now, I needed air.

The chilly night breeze caressed my arms leaving goosebumps everywhere it touched. The moon was bright and full, it should've been beautiful. I haven't been able to appreciate my surroundings lately. Mostly because I see misfortune in all of it.

I am so fucking tired of having to be strong all the time

I just want to be happy.

Not confused

Not hurt

Not stressed

Just happy.

I'm trying my hardest not to act how I feel, but it's like everyone around me is always pining against me. I can't do anything right. I'm alone, I'm the only one that cares about me.

That's such a selfish thing to say, obviously, people have it worse. Look at me, feeling sorry for myself on my private balcony. At least I have a roof over my head for now. I want for nothing. So why do I feel so anxious?

"Victoria."

The voice behind me breathes. The tone was chilling, not because I was scared but because it was unexpected. I don't even know how he got to my home let alone my balcony. I refuse to turn around.

"Axel."

"When I asked you who it was," He pauses, "Why didn't you tell me?"

"Because of who it was, Axel,"

"Now that you know, what do you really think you can do about it?" I frown into the moonlight. I had rehearsed this conversation in my head. Nevertheless, I still didn't know what to say.

"So you're just going to do nothing? Not even contact the police?" He leans against the railing next to me.

"They'd put my father in jail." I run with his scenario, "Then where do I go? My alcoholic mother? Foster care?"

He stays quiet, shaking his head.

"I appreciate your concern," I soften my voice, "I do, but this is my life. This is a waiting game."

"So what am I supposed to do? Knowing that your bastard of a father hits you. How could I possibly just walk away-" He glowers at my balcony door. No doubt itching to run in and talk to my father.

"He doesn't hit me, it was only once," Feeling the old tears on my face, I keep it pointed to the moon.

"No parent should hit their fucking kid hard enough to leave a bright ass bruise," He spins me towards him, "Especially on your face."

His eyes take a second to recognize my wet cheeks, but as soon as he does he brings his hand up. Rubbing my cheek with his thumb.

"Princess-"

"I agree with you," I cut him off, pulling his hand away from my face, "It's wrong you're right,"

"But what the hell am supposed to do about it?" I back away from him, "That's why I didn't tell you, that's why I haven't told anyone. There's nothing that you or anyone can do. All options lead to me being the one that suffers,"

"Cazzate!" He runs his hands through his hair, "Oh mio fottuto Dio,"(Bullshit - Oh my fucking god)

"Don't yell at me in languages I don't understand." I cross my arms at him.

"I'm not yelling at you, Gattina." He sighs, "I just - fuck."(Kitten)

"Just leave it alone." The whimper in my voice must have shown him how I feel because his head snaps to me.

His arms wrap around me and I let them. I breathe in his scent and I relax in his warmth. I tried to wrap up my tears as I laid my head on his shoulder.

"I can't just walk away now that I know your home life. Princess, you flinch when he so much as looks at you. What kind of person would I be if I just ignored that?" He pulls away enough for me to look at him, his hand smoothing my hair.

I keep quiet, not having an answer.

"I swear to God, you better call me if he even so much as bucks at you," Axel finally sighs out.

I nod, even though I don't foresee my father hitting me again.

"Thank you," I whisper, "Looks like you always catch me crying,"

I scoff, trying to lighten the mood.

He shakes his head,

"I'd rather you cry in front of me than alone."

<3

"I haven't seen you wear glasses since the sixth grade," Mia jokes with me as we make our way to lunch.

I decide to wear my glasses today instead of normally settling for my contacts. Partly because I didn't feel like it, but also because my eyes were slightly swollen from crying all last night.

Axel stayed with me long into the night. I told him I was fine, but he insisted on staying. We stayed out on the balcony. Laying on the cold floor and discussing where we wanted our lives to end.

I saw another side of him last night. I definitely have a little more respect for him. Not everybody would care - let alone stay with me. I appreciate him.

"It's refreshing," I smile softly.

"I can understand that."

We fall into a comfortable silence. Once we can see the cafeteria doors, she stops. I look at her questionably. Glancing around, she pulls me into a vacant classroom.

"What the hell-"

"Listen," She cuts me off. I'm taken aback but I stay quiet nonetheless, "How long have we been friends?"

"Two years," I lift a brow, trying to figure out where she's going with this.

"I know we're not as close as we used to be, but I still care about you. We've been holding something from you."

We?

I nod for her to continue.

"It's Liv," Mia states, "She's been - talking - about you, like negatively. When you're not around, they drag you through the mud. I thought they would let up, but last night, during the press conference with your dad. She made a group chat without you. In it, she just talks shit." Mia pulls out her phone, showing me the text messages.

She thinks she's all that

She's so ungrateful, someone needs to talk to her

We need to have a group meeting, she's becoming such a bitch

She's always skipping school, she thinks daddy's money is going to carry her through life

Hateful words flood the page, all about me. If only they knew. If only they cared about knowing. I've always known this group of girls were followers. Most of them probably didn't have a problem with me, but because Olivia isn't happy with me, they aren't.

There's always been two main personalities in this group: Me and Olivia.

I scoff, "Where is she?"

Mia's eye widen, "Vic, no, don't-"

"No, it's bigger than this," I cut her off, "I'm going to deal with this right - fucking - now,"

"Where is she?"

<h1 style="text-align:center">~ Chapter 19 ~</h1>

"Sorry to interrupt."

There Olivia stood, hand on the forearm of Axel Stone and lips only inches apart. I was so furious. I was pissed before I found Olivia, but this only escalated it. I, myself, knew I was jealous in some way. However, as long as I live I will deny it. It was the small affection I had been shown. It's more than I've ever felt in my entire life.

A boy does not have to show me twice he is not interested

"Olivia." I grit out. "Oh what in the entire fuck?"

The situation is so out of pocket, it's funny. She was just telling me how much of a bad person he was and now I catch her cuddled up with him behind the school - next to dumpsters.

The bearing of the teeth was for me to contain my anger. Yet, it only came out more aggressive. My breathing was heightened as the adrenaline rushed through my veins. Memories of the peak of our friendship flow through my brain. After this conversation, we were no longer going to be friends.

"I was slightly busy." She laughs, looking back at Axel.

"What happened to him be a player? You were just telling me how much of a bad person he was,"

"Yeah, this is me showing you."

Only he's not smiling or even looking at her. He's looking at me, face concealed under some blank expression. If I looked a little harder I probably could've figured it out, but he wasn't the one I had business with right now. It was her.

"Fuck him, I'm here for you."

I wave dismissively towards Axel. Walking towards them, discarding him to the side completely.

"I will not stay silent so that you can stay comfortable," I seethe, "You have forgotten that I am not like our other friends. You can manipulate them, but you can not manipulate me."

As former best friends, I knew this fight was going to be lethal. The only problem was that she had shared more with me, than I, her. No one knew me truly. I've always been closed off. She was going to attack me with the things she thought I was. If I'm being honest, that would hurt worse.

She stood there cuddled with the boy she told me was no good. I wanted to punch her. I wanted to wreak havoc, but I again remembered my place. The promise to my father. All I could do was wish my words cut deep enough that it amounted more than any punch could. The goal was to hurt her. The goal was to make her think - reevaluate her life.

"What are you complaining about, this time?" Her eyes rolled, in a way brushing me off as she's had a way of doing.

"The group chat," Recognition glazes her eyes, "You really think those girls wouldn't tell me? Do you truly believe that they have more loyalty to you than me?"

"No, you don't think that. That's why you've been talking about me for months. Trying desperately to get them to side with you."

"I know that." I step closer to her. "The question is: Why?"

"There you fucking go!" She throws her hands up, "Thinking you know every damn thing. I'm sick of it, the girls are sick of it too. We'd planned to talk to you about everything. We've noticed you've changed."

"Damn right I've changed!" I scream back at her.

"What is that supposed to mean?"

"It means I've grown. It means I've matured," I scoff, "Maybe you should try it sometime."

"You've always thought you were better than us-"

"No, Olivia," I cut her off, "You've always thought I was better than you."

"Friendship is every day, not just when it's convenient for you." I can feel my nostrils flare.

"If I lose you as a friend from being honest, then you weren't a good friend," She huffs, crossing her arms. I can still feel Axel's presence behind me. It's like he's the fuel and I'm the fire. His very presence makes my anger flare.

The nerve - the literal audacity

I could only snort, "You're such a fucking bitch."

I turn to walk away. I didn't want to go back to lunch with the other girls and definitely didn't want to go into class. However, I couldn't skip, not at this time.

"So you're just ready to lose a friend?"

My steps didn't falter and my stride didn't slow, "Multiple." I correct her.

"I didn't lose friends, I just realized I never had any."

<3

I was hand mopping the ring at the gym. Today I would try waxing it. This was so the wax would be dry and ready by the fight Friday night.

I wouldn't be attending that one, Friday was my father's little diner.

"Girl, they got you working - breaking a sweat and everything," Athena jokes from the other side of the caged ring. I chuckle along with her.

"But they pay well so it's all good."

I'd felt a certain pair of steely grey eyes on me since I walked into the building. Purposefully not looking anywhere near them. I wasn't even angry anymore, I was tired. Axel had a habit of being inquisitive and I wasn't in the mood for that right now.

"Those glasses look really good on you." Noah smiled at me from VIP.

I return it, pushing them up and going back to scrubbing.

"Are you going to the fight Friday? It's Axel against some four-time champ. It's gonna be really go-"

"Nope." I cut Tyler off, "Do you think this is enough wax? Or should I maybe go for one more coat?"

It was a real question. They were a level higher and had a better view. It also doubled as a conversation changer so it's a win-win.

"It's fine." The sharp voice cuts through all other opinions.

Yet, I still didn't look. Instead, going by his statement I started to buff out the floors. The conversation went back to whatever nonsense this group talked about. I could still feel the eyes on me. I'd had enough, looking up at them with a raised brow.

His stare didn't falter, not even in the slightest. He moved to stand and I tore my gaze away. I finished up the floor quickly, shuffling to the employee room.

Somewhere he wasn't allowed to be

I knew it wouldn't stop him from going in, but this way, if he decided to talk to me it would be in a little bit of privacy.

"So you're not even going to mention what happened today at lunch?" He asks as soon as I hear the lock of the door.

"Mention to whom? You? No, I wasn't."

I try to busy myself, wiping down counters and throwing random things away. Anything to avoid his gaze. I was tired of being emotional in front of him. I would no longer allow it. He has been officially put on the - no emotion list - it was bound to happen.

"So you cry on my shoulder only hours ago and now we're back to square one?" He frowns, I can hear it in his voice.

"Oh, go to hell, we never left square one," I finally turn to face him, "And about last night, if you came to throw it back in my face. Don't worry. It won't be happening again."

"I'm not- listen, Victoria," He sighs loudly.

I was being difficult. We've already been through this routine, only this time. I wouldn't come running back to him and apologize.

"I just saw you cuss out your best friend," He states, "Are you- were you jealous?"

"Oh, so, you knew we were friends?" I bring my lips to a tight line, scoffing. "Clearly the argument wasn't about you at all,"

"It honestly wasn't what it looked like,"

"Well, it looked like if I had arrived five seconds later I would've walked in on a heated make-out session," I don't look at him, fumbling with some cleaning supplies. "You're telling me that's not what it was?"

"I didn't kiss her,"

"No, I interrupted you,"

"I wasn't going to-"

"Listen, that's not the point-" I blurt, "Sorry to burst your bubble of pride, but I wasn't upset about you kissing her. I don't care who you fuck, Axel. I really don't."

I drop the cleaning supplies, turning to him.

"If you think this save-a-hoe bullshit will get you laid then I suggest you might wanna try it on another girl." I push past him to open the door.

"Angel-"

"I didn't stutter."

Chapter 20

I was staring at my reflection in the mirror

I was in my pretty red dress, my hair and makeup was done. I looked pretty - I looked nice. So then why am I staring at the mirror so intently?

The feign happiness that sets on my face, broke my own heart. It wasn't the expression necessarily. It was more of the fact that I knew I was about to greet over a hundred people and none of them would notice. I feel as if I'm on display and invisible at the same time. I'm seen by everyone but truly seen by no one.

Is it selfish of me to want someone to ask me if I'm okay?

Is it juvenile to want to be swept off my feet and given a fairytale?

I shouldn't feel like this. I have the ideal life. I've never had to worry about money or food. I beat myself up about that all the time. Sometimes Olivia's words would get to me. Maybe I am self-centered, inconsiderate even. Being born with the dream and only wanting to get out of it.

I shake my head, today, I couldn't have any desires for myself. It would only make faking this whole thing harder. I grab my handbag and walk down the stairs.

Nod and smile would be my go-to move this evening

<3

"Miss Beckette, Miss Beckette!" A report shouts as I walk into the venue. I smile and wave at the man, letting him at least know I saw him.

My father and his mistress rode separately so they could make their grand entrance seconds after mine. I was to go straight to the head table and keep my mouth shut. As my father explained to me earlier today.

There was a dinner rehearsal late last night. It was extremely extensive and only between us and the staff. My father made me skip school so my first appearance today would be here, at this dinner. Not that I'm upset about that. I had some people at school to avoid.

I sat at my table in front of the guest with a smile. I prayed my father would show up quickly so I wouldn't look so awkward anymore.

"Can we have all guests be seated as the couple makes their entrance?" A voice over the intercom comes in. Everybody that was socializing or drinking at the bar quickly shifted to their assigned seats and stared at the double doors.

Almost as if on beat, the doors bust open. The couple in question standing arm in arm. A classic melody plays and they smile while making their way down the aisle. I heard a sea of 'aws' and 'They're so cutes', as I could only bite my cheek. No one knew that they argued like cats and dogs when alone. They weren't even married yet.

From what I could gather of the argument last night, the same female reporter from the conference has come to put a little hole in their honeymoon phase. I hadn't noticed at the conference, but I recalled after the argument. The reporter was the same woman that stood next to my father in our kitchen only weeks ago. Carol seems to think they've been sleeping together.

I'd say she's smart to assume so

My father decided to settle on a red hearted suit, and Carol went with a long loose fitted red gown.

"Thank you, close friends and trusted business partners." My father makes his statement at the podium. His mistress coming to sit next to me. She doesn't look at me and I don't look at her.

"Today we've come together to celebrate a new chapter in my life. After one love ends, another one begins," He turns his head to smile over at his soon-to-be wife. "I now have two loves."

I guess the second love was supposed to be me, I smile lightly at my father.

"I won't bother you with all the reasons why I love my darling Carol- we'd be here all night," The crowd laughs and my father's poor joke, "But my daughter wanted to say a few things before we release you to the dining hall."

I walk over to where my father stood, he guides me by the small of my back to the podium.

"Don't fuck it up." He leaves a kiss on my temple and goes to sit in the seat next to Carol. I resist the urge to roll my eyes, plastering a smile on my face.

"It's been a long time since I've seen either of my parents happy," I start off, "They've worked incredibly hard to stay together to have a united family,

I know that. However, all I want for our family is for both of them to be happy, even if that means separately."

I take a deep breath, trying to push down the vile at the back of my throat. "I'm excited to get to know Ms. Carol, she's an amazing woman, who I think will do great by my dad,"

"As Mark Anthony states: 'I found you without looking and loved you without trying', I hope one day we will all be able to live by those words. Everyone deserves to love," The crowd nods in mutual agreement.

"Thank you." I nod and move back to my seat.

I needed to sit. I felt sick to my stomach. How could I be so deceitful? I hate lying. Beyond this setting, I refused to do it. I'm constantly reevaluating how I feel so I won't lie to myself. In order to be level-headed, I have to be in complete control of my emotions. Which requires honesty.

"Let dinner begin!"

I didn't eat.

I wasn't hungry. That and the dress I had on wouldn't look too flattering if I tore into those jumbo shrimp like I really wanted to. I instead walked around and introduced myself.

"How is it, Mrs. Richards?"

"That steak looks so good, Mr. Owen."

"How's the granddaughter, Ms. Haynes?"

This was really the time I'd show off the southern charm I had been brought up with. Polite smiles and gentle waves became the routine for the next hour.

"Excuse me, honey, Victoria?" A strong voice catches my attention from behind. I turn with a smile, trying to recall the names of the couple before I spoke.

"Mr. and Mrs. Saunters! How was dinner?" The blonde hair and dazzling blue eyes were a dead giveaway. They were identical to their son.

Speaking of which I hadn't seen, not like I was looking-

"It was just above wonderful, honey. We wanted to see where your father was?" I nodded, gesturing to the bar where my father stood talking to a few other business partners.

The room suddenly felt crowded, everybody at this time was moving around and starting to get drinks. The atmosphere was lifting into a hectic one and I most certainly was not feeling it. I tried to find a bathroom, finding some stairs instead.

This is totally a sleeping beauty moment

I followed the stairs that were dimly lit with yellow lights. The bright red bathroom signs got a sigh of relief out of me. I followed it all the way to the top, starting to regret my choice of heels. They were cute, but not practical. There certainly wasn't this much standing at the practice dinner.

At the top of the stairs, there was the bathroom but also a set of glass doors. I looked between the two. A small black figure catches my eye from the glass doors.

Glass doors it is

I push through them, the cool night air chilling every exposed part of my body. It was relieving though. The stars plastered the night sky beautifully. I leaned against the stone railing of the balcony. There was no longer a moon in sight.

The dark figures seemed to be a raven, my raven. Yet, as soon as I set my eyes on it, it flew away. The dark feathers of the bird blended into the starlit sky.

"One day,"

A voice soothes behind me, making me jump slightly.

"Love will come in the form of somebody who wants to give more than take," The boy continues walking over to where I stood at the balcony.

"And you will know why love is rare." He finished, blue eyes blaring into mine.

Lucas Saunters

"Mark Anthony," I smile softly.

"Mark Anthony." He nods.

"Beautiful speech, by the way," He adds, "You've handled your parent's divorce so well. I don't know if I could do that,"

"I didn't even know you were in there to hear it," I chuckle lightly.

"I don't really like these social events," He smiles shyly, "You seem to be amazing at them though. You charm absolutely everyone,"

"You're telling me-" I turn to him. "-that the Captain of the football team, golden boy of the school, can't handle a small dinner party?" I smile teasingly at him.

"I would hardly call this small." He snorts back.

We fall into a comfortable silence. Looking up at the stars was all the conversation that was needed.

"You have really pretty eyes," Lucas randomly states.

I shift my head to look at him and I see that he was no longer looking at the night sky. I turn back quickly, trying my hardest to suppress my blush.

"The stars can make anything appear beguiling."

***

< Her dinner dress >

~ Chapter 21 ~

"So how did the fight go?"

I asked Athena first this Monday morning. All weekend I had been hiding out. I turned my phone off, and I just drove. The only time I looked at my phone was when I wanted to find my way back home.

Even when I looked at the phone I hadn't gotten a text from Athena about the fight, seeing as the fight was supposed to be a good one, something seemed off. I hated myself for being so concerned. I had just fought with Axel and I'd intended to wane myself off from seeing him.

Athen gives me a sullen smile, "Axel won."

Oh, good

"But, it was a tough fight. That boy gave him a run for his money. I haven't talked to Axel since that Friday before the match after Axel got his money, he bolted."

I pause, "Well, i-is he hurt?"

I swayed on if I should've even asked. It really isn't my place and I can tell that Axel probably didn't want people knowing about it.

"I'm pretty sure I saw a few cuts when they called him as the winner." She looks at me, I know she can tell I'm concerned.

Ring

"I'll see you at lunch, okay?" She shoots me a soft smile before turning to walk behind the school. Most likely to skip class. I also smile at the rest of the guys waiting for her.

"Hey?" I grab her attention before she walks off,

"Can you send me Axel's address?"

It wasn't my place

I had just gotten on him about him coming to my rescue - as dumb as that sounds. I would be a complete hypocrite if I went to check upon him. I feel like in some way I owe this visit to him.

I do owe this visit to him

He could be mad at me all he wanted but I was going to at least knock on his front door.

It's like an urge - which is crazy - he makes me so angry it constricts my chest. The mere thought of him pressed against the brick wall with Olivia makes me burning from head to toe. How I let myself get so infatuated with him this quickly is beyond me and frankly, it's embarrassing.

Nonetheless, every time I'm not busy I find myself thinking of him. He can be funny when he wants to. Sometimes he's hilarious. When he's with his friends I get to see that light-hearted part of him. So, why? Why does he get me so angry? Why can't he just make it easy for me?

If anything he could use a good punching; something to water down that ego of his.

WHY do I need to check on hi-

"Miss Beckette," A sharp voice cuts at me from the front of the room.

"Yes, Ms. Boucher?"

I couldn't skip school or else we would end up in another crying session on my balcony. However, as soon as those last bells ring my car will be headed in the direction of the address Athena sent me.

"Care to tell me what I just said?"

I look around the room, I hadn't heard her. Everyone looked at me, but not in a mocking way. This was a daily thing. Someone was bound to be picked on in her class and I guess today, like many other days, I was it.

Lucas catches my eyes from the front of the classroom, he smiles and mouths to me.

group project

I wink in appreciation returning my gaze to Ms. Boucher, "You were explaining our group project," I state calmly.

"If you continue with this behavior your grade will suffer," It already is. "However, that is correct. You will be allowed to pick your partners."

"People who got an A- and above on the last quiz get first pick," She trails off walking behind her desk, "Starting with... Mr. Saunters!"

Lucas's eyes scan the room before landing on me, "I'll pick Victoria."

"You sure?"

He nods.

"Also class," She raises her head, "If your partner is not doing their fair share, you can come to me privately and we'll work something out."

Really? I don't think that was necessary

I roll my eyes, turning to face the window again. Sadly my little friend wasn't there. Nevertheless, the bright and beautiful morning sun was always a sight within itself.

"She gets on you pretty hard, huh?" Luca's bright smile greets me as he sits in front of me.

"She gets on everybody pretty hard, no hard feelings," I state simply, turning my body to face him.

I didn't want him to think that I actually don't do anything. I definitely did my fair share in projects, in fact, most of the time I did the whole thing. I don't usually mind though, I like doing things my way.

"Yeah, I know." He sighs, "That shouldn't be allowed, teachers aren't supposed to make students feel bad about themselves."

I can't help but let a smile peek at the side of my lip. It was cute how he cared. Genuine reactions are always refreshing to be around.

"So what is this project about?" I shift the conversation.

"We need to plan a trip to America, then make a brochure all in french."

I sigh audibly, which he chuckles softly at.

"Come on, we're going to have the best brochure in the classroom, I mean, just look around." He laughs.

He was sort of right, everyone else seemed to either not be doing the project or not know what's going on. It wasn't like these kids were dumb. It really does take a good teacher to make a good class and right now none of us are really feeling the teacher.

"We can get started today, after school,"

I shake my head, "I'm busy today, but I'm good tomorrow."

"I have football practice tomorrow, but that's fine with me as long as you don't mind waiting," He shrugs.

"I just have to be to work by seven, anything before that is totally cool with me," I shoot him a tight-lipped smile.

"You work? I would think that with your father-"

"Yeah, I understand," I cut him off, "I just want my own money, you know?"

He probably didn't know, his parents being of a rich status like my father. Lucas probably had no desire to work. His father was gearing him to run the company after he retired. Lucas most likely didn't want to do that. What did he want to do then? A pro-football player would be my guess.

I didn't care, I wasn't one to judge. If Lucas wanted to play football professionally, that's cool. If Lucas wanted to live off his parent's money, that's cool as well. Not everybody had my situation and vice versa. I couldn't speak for anybody else.

"That's very admirable,"

I wanted to snort at his word choice, but I kept it to myself.

"Yeah, something like that."

<3

I was staring at the tall house. It was pretty. A traditional-styled southern home. It was rather nice as well. I wonder what Axel's parents do? I've never asked and Axel's never mentioned it.

I get out, breathing in deeply as I approach the pretty dark green door. It recently has occurred to me that I don't actually have Axel's number.

Whenever he needed to get in touch with me he would text me through Blaze or Athena's number.

I push the doorbell, knocking softly three times. My breathing shallows.

He doesn't even want to see me

I take a few steps back, trying to control my sudden anxiety. I was not going to turn away, I was going to at least set eyes on him before leaving. If that means I have to stay here for hours, so be it.

The door is thrown open, Axel stands shirtless at the entrance. Although I would love to gawk at those abs of his, my eyes were drawn to his face. More specifically his eye.

"Axel," I gasp.

He raises a brow at me, "Did you need something?"

"You can't just leave open wounds untreated," I ignore his questions, he wasn't beat up bad and I didn't want to make him feel like he was.

"I didn't realize you became a doctor," He scoffs at me, leaning against the frame.

"You're bleeding," I push through him to get into the house, "Where's your first aid?"

"It's blood, not nuclear waste. Chill out," His sarcasm is just flowing today. I find a rag, whiskey, and some spiderman bandaids.

"Please, sit down." I tighten my jaw. He just looks at me, shaking his head, he sits down.

I start to dip the rag in whiskey, then dab it lightly on his cheek. That seemed to be the large gash. The tension in the room was suffocating, I could tell he was upset with me. Honestly, I was upset with myself. I'm always acting off of predetermined feelings. I'll dwell on something all day then act upon this feeling that I've made up. However, I promised in the workroom that I was not going to apologize. I did plan on keeping that.

"No one helped you with this?" I frown moving to the small cuts on his lips. I knew it stung, but Axel was taking it like a champ.

"I didn't ask anyone too." He all but growls out the words. I sigh deeply.

"I know- are you-," I bite my cheek, frustrated. "Why didn't you- did you feel like I wouldn't care?"

He frowns, "Care about what?"

About you being hurt. I feel like if I hadn't yelled at you, you would've come to my house, have me fix you up. I owe you this check-up-

No, I couldn't say that.

I tread to the kitchen, getting some ice for the bruising under his eyes. "Your injury,"

I simply state, wanting to explain so much more.

"No, why would I think you'd care?" I can tell he's getting aggravated.

It seems like no matter where I take the conversation, I'm stepping on a land mine. I wanted to know how he felt about our last conversation.

"I-"

"You didn't stutter, remember? I heard you loud and clear the first time. We never left square one," He mocks my previous hurtful statements. I look away from him, embarrassed that I even thought having that conversation with him was a good idea.

"Can you blame me?"

"Yes!" He grabs my waist, pushing me against the kitchen counter,

"I can."

~ Chapter 22 ~

"You do this shit every other week!"

Axel's grey eyes blazing into mine. His face was merely inches away from mine, yet I wasn't threatened. I have been yearning to hear how he feels, as I feel half of our conversations are one-sided.

"One day you're vulnerable the next day you're pushing me off. If I wasn't so fucking hard-headed, we'd probably never talk," He lifts me to the counter, placing his hands on either side of me.

"You make it so fucking hard to care about you!"

This line hit, not because it was hurtful, but because it's eye-opening. Not once did it cross my mind that Axel was genuine about caring. I had been pushing him away.

"I know!" I yell back at up, my hands go to press against my temple as I can feel a trainwreck of a headache coming along.

"Axel-," I cut myself off with an aggressive sigh, "Fuck."

"This shouldn't be so goddamn hard!" I push him away so that I could pace across the kitchen floor. I needed air, I needed to breathe.

"I'm living a constant lie and I have been for years. Press conference after press conference and social gathering after school gathering. I fake this perfect life," I continue to pace the floor as Axel leans on his counters with his arms crossed. "Somehow the only person that notices is you,"

"And I can't figure it out," I pause and face him.

"You can't hide it from me, princess," His tone is calmer now, his features have softened.

"I know," I look down. "That's what scares me."

Hands pick up my face, I meet Axel's eye. It was only at this moment where my emotions weren't conflicted.

"How many times do I have to tell you I care about you?" He chuckles humorlessly, "How many different ways do you want me to say it?"

"You don't even know me,"

"I don't need to."

I try to wring my face out of his hands, he doesn't budge. "But Olivia-"

"Came onto me literally thirty seconds before you turned the corner,"

"Oh, bullshit," I scrunch my face. "You had her pinned against the wall,"

"I was leaning on the wall, yes," He rolls his eyes. "Pinning her, no,"

Who is he lying to? I saw it with my own eyes.

"Anyways, She only talked about you the entire time," He sighs, "Such a turn off,"

I push him again and he lets me. "I hate you so much,"

"Don't worry, doll, no one can keep up with me like you can," He shines a boyish smile.

Then there was silence, me looking at him and him looking at me. I was searching his eyes for any sign of deception. See if he was lying, it would make this situation so much easier. For years I've just wanted someone that looked slightly lower than the surface. Now that I had it, I was scared.

I was scared because he is the one person that I don't think I'd be okay with losing. Scared because I have to fight logic with him. Knowing that the only thing I want to do is melt into all that is Axel Stone.

However, Axel is a son of a bitch- and nothing is ever that easy.

"I don't care what you say, sweetheart, you can push me all you want," We were forehead to forehead, "I won't leave you alone,"

"Are you flirting or trying to start a fight?" I smile softly.

"Hopefully both."

He leans in, his lips brush past mine shooting electricity throughout my entire face. His breath fans my skin in the most pleasurable ways. I was completely overwhelmed with Axel Stone. I was putty in his hands.

At this moment, I'd be his if he asked

Lethal lust - some might call it.

"Dude, Noah farted in the car and refused to let down the windows!"

Loud voices enter the house as Axel's lips were negative point five seconds away from mine. An annoyed sigh emits from the back of Axel's throat and I jump back trying to compose myself.

"Hi, Victoria."

"What's up, Tori?"

"How's it going, gorgeous?"

Noah, Kaiden, and Tyler enter with greetings to me. I shoot them all a smile as I avoid eye contact with Axel. I'm afraid if I were to look at him right now, I would forget my manners and continue our actions from earlier.

"Y'all are here early," Axel states bitterly as he turns to meet the boys.

"Jace decided to go home after football practice today," Kaiden drops down on the island stool.

"Why?" Axel frowns slightly, eyes drifting from me for only seconds.

"He and his father need to speak about graduation plans."

The answers were vague. I had a feeling it was because they knew an outsider was still in the room. The outsider being me. I understood completely, I definitely wasn't going to pry and in all honesty, I didn't really care. It wasn't my business.

Through their conversation, I took the time to actually take in my surroundings. Little trinkets of boy possessions litter the home. In a way that this almost looked like a bachelor pad instead of a family home.

"You live together?" I totally interrupted their conversation. I didn't mean to. I was thinking out loud.

"Yes."

"Is that why you fight? To pay the bills?" The question was directed at Axel.

"You hit the nail on the head, darling." I lock eyes with him.

He definitely expected more questions, but I wouldn't ask them. Not now, not in front of the other boys. I just simply nod.

"Yup, sorry Tori, not everybody has a rich father," Kaiden winked. He was joking and I wasn't offended. The joke wasn't the kind you laughed at.

"Want mine?" I retort right back.

"Cute,"

"Aren't I?"

Kaiden I am just as quick-witted as you, if not more.

"Damn, I like you."

I give him a playful wink. "Well, I have to get back to my rich father,"

"I'll walk you out," Axel states quickly, guiding me out of the kitchen.

I gather my keys, trying to contain my rapid breathing as Axel leads me out of the house by the small of my back. If only the boys had come in a few seconds later-

"Ignore Kaiden," Axel talks as we reach my car. "He doesn't mean any harm."

"No offense taken," I wave Axel off. Kaiden was a jerk, I knew that. That's just the way he is. I personally know he didn't mean it in a malicious way so I wouldn't take it like that.

I start to get my car, Axel scoffs loudly, "What? No goodbye kiss?"

The smirk could be heard through his voice. I couldn't wipe the smile off my face even if I wanted to.

"You can kiss my ass,"

He chuckles, "Nothing would make me happier."

I laugh along with him, settling myself in the driver's seat. From an outsider's view, we probably looked like two goofballs just smiling at each other. I couldn't help it, I was giddy. Axel leans against the car with one arm.

"I'll see you tomorrow?"

"You might," I smiled widely up at him.

"There's a party Friday," He starts, "I'll pick you up at eight."

It would've sounded sleazy if any other guy said it like that. However, when it came from Axel I was more than ecstatic to go. I was no stranger to having a good time. Getting dressed up and dancing was kind of my thing. I also had new dresses still sitting in bags in my closet that I couldn't exactly wear to school.

"Pick me up at ten."

I close the door, getting ready to drive off. Axel had started to tread to the door when I rolled down the window to speak one last time.

"Hey!" Axel turns around, "Tell Kaiden to stop calling me 'Tori'-"

"It's a terrible nickname."

~ Chapter 23 ~

"Your mother called."

The words echoed throughout my otherwise silent kitchen. Our home had become so empty that as soon as he opened his mouth, I could smell the whiskey on his breath. My front was facing the stairs as my father sits at the island facing my back.

I let out a long sigh, "When?"

"While you were at school, today." He sips on his glass, the sound also echoing off the marble countertops.

"You can just text me the number," I brush him off, starting up the stairs. Conversations with my father did not need to be extensive; especially not while he drinks.

"She called to say she's put herself in rehab," He ignored me, "She wanted to talk to you before she had to put her phone away for sixty days,"

I turn to meet his gaze, "That's amazing,"

"Victoria," He cautioned, "I don't want you in contact with her. She will only bring bad news."

His lips were tight and his eyebrows furrowed. I can't help but wonder how he justifies his thoughts. Does he even think over it? Does he think of anyone but himself?

I knew the answer to the second one: No.

"You want to keep me away from my mother?"

"You can hardly call her that,"

"As if you're any better," I scoff, "I'd take her over you any day."

He shot up quickly with my sharp words. His whiskey glass abandoned, but his breath was just as strong.

"You better fix your lips before I pop you in them,"

"I know," I back down, "I know. I'm aware of the drill father."

He whips back around to his decanter set. Lifting some Jack Daniels into a new glass cup. Anger came off of him in waves, from his head to his expensive shoes I could see his growing aggravation towards me.

Did I care? No, no I didn't.

"You can't keep me away from her," I state as I head up the stairs. I quickly perk up again before he could run up the stairs and pop me.

"But I'll make sure not to get caught."

<3

"You can't just keep ignoring her in Bio, eventually you two are going to have to talk," Mia states knowingly.

She was right, I couldn't just keep hanging out with Jace - Kaiden's brother - and his friends in the back of the class. Olivia and I hadn't even made eye contact since our fight outside. I also hadn't attempted to talk to our mutual friends. The only people I've been in contact with from our little group is Mia.

"I'm just going to let it play out," I state simply, "Let the pieces of the puzzle fall where they may,"

"Alright, bye beautiful," She kisses my cheek treading to her car, "Text me about how you and the golden boy's date go." She wiggles her brow.

I roll my eyes. This definitely wasn't going to be a date. I actually started to dread waiting for Lucas to finish practice. The football players scare me, they're all big and not very smart. Which is a toxic combination.

Shit, I forgot my french notes in my locker

I sigh loudly, turning on my heels to jog back to my locker. It wasn't that long of a walk, but that wasn't the point. It's just inconvenient. I gather the notebook and secure the lock. Another loud sigh emits from my throat. These next few hours were going to be full of awkward conversations and uncomfortable silences.

"Victoria?"

The voice of the one boy I had been subconsciously looking for all day brought a smile to my face. I turn in his direction.

"What are you doing here?" I joke, most of the time Axel doesn't even show up to school, so why the hell was he here after hours?

"I was about to ask you the same thing," He chuckles, "I've got detention. What are you doing here?"

My face drops, "I have a french project with Lucas Saunters, so I'm just waiting for him to get out of practice,"

"Ah, that's going to be awkward," He snorts, "Let me walk you to the field, I'm not in any rush to get to detention,"

"Aren't you already late?" We start to walk towards the school doors. I move to check my phone.

"Yeah, so?"

I just chuckle softly at him, he was truly a bad boy at heart. We start to walk in comfortable silence. The fresh air and dazzling afternoon sun had my complete and utter attention. The click of a camera attracts my attention back to Axel - more like Axel's phone - which was shoved in my face.

"Can I help you?" I laugh, pushing his camera away from my face.

"The sun was pretty," Axel looks offended that I would even question his motives, "But the next one can be of you if it would make you feel better,"

"No thanks."

The bleachers were now in front of us, I can see the football players doing suicides across the field. My lungs burn for them; I've never been an athletic person.

Axel places his hand on my waist, his lips next to my ear.

"You know," He whispers, "We could go under those bleachers and finish what we started yesterday."

His offer was tempting, a lot more tempting than waiting under this hot sun. However, who would I be to give in that easily?

"Maybe you can dream about all the things we would've done, tonight." I pat his cheek, pulling away from his hands.

"I'll catch you later, Stone,"

"I'll see you tonight, sexy."

I try to shake my smile as I pick a semi-shading spot on the bleachers. I can hear the coach blowing the whistle and yelling with no end from where I sat.

I almost immediately make eye contact with Lucas, his bright blue eyes sparkled in the rays of sun. He shoots me a smile before turning back to his team. His draw from the conversation leaving them to search where his gaze landed. Of course, all of their eyes ended up on me.

I give them a small wave, feeling awkward under all of their stares. They push and shove each other with laughs present on their face, as boys do.

"You can come home with me tonight, baby girl," One of the brunettes shouts from the field.

"Yeah, stop fucking with Saunters and ride with the winning team." Another one adds, both of them averagely attractive. I wiggled in my seat to get comfortable on the hard metal.

This is going to be one long-ass practice

~ Chapter 24 ~

"Sorry about that."

Lucas jogs to where I sat in the bleachers. I give him a tight-lipped smile checking my watch. We had a good two hours before I had to make my way into work.

"It's all good," I grab all my things. "Do you normally drop the ball that much during practice or do I just have the pleasure of witnessing a bad day?"

I tease him with a smile, trying to ease any uncomfortable silence these few hours might hold. He chuckles deeply at my comment, shooting me a playful glare.

"I see you're quite the comedian,"

"Call it a talent."

No matter how hard I tried to avoid it, the uncomfortable silence set in as we walked to the sitting area by the trees. He didn't make a motion to fix it and I didn't want to be the only one talking, so here we are - stuck.

I pulled out everything I thought we would need for the project, Lucas pulls out nothing. I flipped to the assignment she posted, Lucas continues to just watch me.

"Have you thought about some of the things you want to do?" I speak up again, he meets my eye.

"Yeah, I looked into it last night." He pulls out his phone, fingers dancing over the screen quickly before sliding it over to me.

"Holy- Oh my God,"

Lucas had our project skillfully laid out on the notes of his phone. Taking into account how little he had to work with, the project looked awesome. I immediately start to feel bad about being annoyed at his lack of effort. He didn't have to pull anything out, he'd already finished it.

"Lucas, I- you didn't have to," I manage to stutter, "I would've totally done my part,"

"I know, I know, but I had free time last night," He waves me off, "French is my favorite subject anyway,"

"Really? Is there a reason?" I didn't want to just leave. There was only one reason we were hanging out right now. The project was done and there truly was no reason for me to be sitting under the trees with the handsome football player anymore.

"French is my native language, it's the only thing that comes naturally to me in school,"

I nod my head in understanding. There was a rumor about three years ago that Lucas had traveled all around the world and wasn't originally from America. That was also another reason why all the girls had flocked to his likeness.

I sigh, "If it's any consolation, I think you project you did, all by yourself, looks incredible,"

"I appreciate that."

Again, with the awkward silence. This time was slightly different from the first. Lucas was looking at me and I was switching my gaze from him to the trees behind him. The sun was still very bright, showing no signs of setting anytime soon. His blue eyes were at their peak under the embrace of the light.

I was trying to enjoy the moment with the cute boy in front of me, but my mind had no control. My thoughts drifted to what grey eyes would look like under the beautiful sun's rays. My heart did something similar to jumping jacks when I remembered that I would see him at work.

"I really like your eyes." Lucas' comment shoots through my ear, wraps around my brain, and squeezes out of my conscience.

"Oh, please," I snort, "Everyone wants blue eyes,"

"Blues eyes are simply a mutation," He retorts back.

"Isn't that what makes them special?"

He looks at me, "That's a good way of looking at it."

I shrug, gathering my stuff. I had a good mind to leave before the conversation ran dry again.

"There's always a contrary side to beliefs, I'm glad I could share mine with you," I say in some sort of dry sarcasm.

"I'll walk you to your car, I have to stay a little longer with the team," He shoots that bright smile at me, taking my bag off my hands and carrying all my things.

I, again, feel bad for not giving him all the attention he was giving me. I should give him a chance. I wasn't dating Axel, I had no loyalty to him. It's never been like me to not have options. I hadn't dated anyone in high school let alone my entire life. Lucas most likely won't change that, but maybe a friendship could come out of it.

I was overthinking, the boy had only complimented my eyes

"When is your next game?" I was trying to be nonchalant, the last thing I wanted him to think was that I was another one of his fangirls.

"Friday, why? Were you thinking about going?"

"I was thinking about it, but there's a party Friday night, so it doesn't look like I'll be able to make it,"

"Party?" He repeated, amused, "I didn't take you for a party girl,"

"I didn't take you as a sucky football player,"

"Oh, come on, I dropped the ball once!"

He was right, I was busting his balls only because he was hyped to the extreme. I had to contain multiple giggle fits as I saw him fumble on the field.

What? That was the only entertaining thing about the whole two-hour-long practice.

We made our way to my car, soft smiles and shy goodbyes were the last of our little project outing. I hopped into my car with a long sigh, pulling out my phone for the first time since hanging out with Lucas.

Surprisingly, I had a message from the grey-eyed boy I had just been day-dreaming about:

I suppress a smile while answering and pull out of the school parking lot.

Hopefully work would be more fulfilling today.

<3

"It's my favorite, baddie!"

Athena sings as I walk into the gym, I embrace her into a tight hug. I truly love this girl, she enjoys my company, and I sure as hell, enjoy hers.

"What tasks do you have for me today?"

"It'll be an easy day because there isn't any fight this week so just look busy and everything will be fine,"

I nod, "I don't have a problem with that."

I grab a rag and some random bottle of cleaning supplies. I had to physically stop myself from looking for the one person I really wanted to see. I walked around the gym talking to a few regular customers and wiping down a few things that looked dirtier than they should be.

"Damn, back so soon?"

The voice I had been looking for, sounded behind me. I let a smile grace my face but shook it away before I turning to look at him.

"It's been two hours since the last time I saw you," I deadpan.

"So," Axel leans against the wall. "Did your golden boy try anything? I don't see any hickeys,"

I shoot him a sharp look, "He was the perfect gentlemen, you should take notes,"

"Oh really now?" His eyebrows lift.

"Yes, he pulled out my chair, carried my things, complimented me. He was very nice,"

I may have exaggerated the extent of our time together. I was just trying to ruffle Axel up. After all, what was I supposed to tell him? That every minute between conversations grew silent and awkward? Or maybe I should've mentioned that every time I found the slightest bit of attraction to Lucas, he would pop into my mind and erase all of that?

"Nice? Sounds boring,"

"You would think that wouldn't you?" My voice was testy, whether seductive or teasing I couldn't figure out. It was a nice mixture of both.

"You would know, wouldn't you, angel?"

"That's right,"

"You're not any better,"

I quip a brow at his suggestion, he continues.

"Well, I remember the first time I saw you," He steps closer, "How you blatantly ignored my presence then winked at me on your way out,"

"I was trying to mind my business," I roll my eyes playfully, "But you were staring extremely hard,"

"You were intriguing,"

"Not to mention insanely gorgeous," I tease, waving a finger at him. "Ethereal even,"

"Oh, I didn't forget. How could I?"

I cut my eyes to him. Before pretending to clean something.

"Smooth guy,"

"The smoothest."

Chapter 25

AXEL'S POV

I was staring at a picture on my phone. It held a beauty looking off into an empty parking lot, sun bouncing off over her glistening skin. It amazed me that I had even gotten to see that in person let alone capture a picture of it. It was now my favorite picture.

"What do you think his infatuation with her is?" Noah runs a hand through his hair, sighing loudly.

"I don't know, but I'm going to find out," I gritted, "He always seems to be around, especially around her. The interest isn't mutual. Most of the time I'm the one pointing out his presence."

The group pauses, all sitting in the VIP area of the gym. Victoria had left a few minutes ago, she gave me no sign that her project with Saunters went bad so I was worried right now.

I've personally never liked Lucas. He's always been phony to me. I told Jace to keep an eye on him, he sees him more than I do.

"Do you think it has something to do with Mr. Beckette?" Taylor's question hung in the air, no one made a move to answer it.

I didn't tell anyone about Victoria's parental issues. I went as far as deleting the texts from Athena's phone after our conversation. However, they knew that Mr. Beckette was very powerful in his field of business. That's why we were trying desperately to avoid him being elected Major.

I'd thought about using Victoria to help, but I couldn't do that to her. I wouldn't be able to sleep at night.

If Victoria's father got Major, the life I've been accustomed to for eight months would change drastically. His election would change everything.

"It better not," I was the one that answered.

That was a good question though, that's the first thing we need to find out. It wouldn't be outside of Beckette's power to have his daughter followed. Would he really choose a high school student to do it though? I guess the better question is would Lucas really do that? Beckette's playing chess and we're playing checkers.

"Keep an eye out, " I cut the conversation short.

"Yeah you fucking better," Athena's sharp voice sounds from the door, "Victoria is a good person. If she gets hurt, it's all on you."

Trust me, I know

<3

"There he is,"

Taylor points at the golden boy's Audi pulling into a parking space. I pull the cigarette from my lips, snarling at its cliche entirety.

"Talk to him," The words fall with the cigarette smoke.

Taylor smiles while walking over to their table. I didn't care what the conversation was about, but I wanted to make my presence known. I needed to let Saunters know he was on my radar.

I go back to scanning the school's yard. I couldn't help but seek out one person in the crowd. It finally hit me in the morning, before class, she wouldn't be here. I stifle a smile while stomping out my cigarette.

Letting my feet guide me to where I know she would be, I have to shake my head at myself. Since when did I become such a fucking pansy? Miss Victoria Beckette has me wrapped around her pretty little finger and she wasn't even trying.

I'm infatuated with her. I'm okay with admitting that to myself and myself only. Nothing more than that would come of this. Once I graduated, I would move to Cali and sign with a random fighting league. I would leave this life behind, I would everything behind.

With the opening of the library doors, Victoria sat on a bench by the window. Her nose deep into some textbooks.

Such a nerd

I made my way over to her. The library was absolutely empty besides us and the librarian.

"What kind of nerd studies before school?" I snatch the textbook out of her lap, it seemed to be a french textbook.

But I wouldn't know, I don't speak french.

"A nerd that doesn't study after school, now may I have it back?" She perches her lips at me, small dimples at her cheeks.

"You take french? Tell me something." I sit down beside her, handing the textbook back.

"I don't know anything, that's why I'm studying,"

Well put, well put

She continued to read her textbook and ignore me. That didn't bother me one bit, I took the time to take in her outfit. A black turtle neck and a jean skirt, damn, she doesn't even have to try to be sexy. I wonder if she knows that? The thought excites me about Friday.

"Have you gone shopping for a dress Friday?" I tease.

"I already have one,"

"Are you just going to keep ignor-"

"You smell of cigarettes," She scrunches her nose, eyes leaving the textbook pages, "If they catch you smoking on school grounds that's an automatic expulsion, you know that right?"

"Being expelled would be one of the better things right now," I smirk at her.

"Right, forgot." Her eyes return to the pages.

She could be so frustrating at times. I shouldn't have to fight this hard for her attention. One second she could be on my kitchen counter centimeters from my lips the next she could be sitting right next to me and paying me no attention. It was a game and I was determined to win.

I wasn't much of a klepto, but I might just have to steal this one's heart.

She lets out a frustrated sigh, shifting around next to me. The book was now on the bench and her back was against a bookshelf. Her hands were tugging at her roots, her feet framing the textbook on the bench.

I muffle my chuckle with a cough, causing her to glare up at me.

"Doll, what are you so stressed about?" I give in and ask.

"No matter how hard I study, French and I just don't connect," She frowns, "I've been studying the French language for forever, but it doesn't matter. I'm just not one of those people that can learn a language,"

"Why are you even taking French? All you need is two credits to graduate,"

"It looks good on college applications,"

I shoot her a pointed look, "Who are you lying to?"

"Okay, it was my father's suggestion, but I agree with him!" She assured.

"Well, what's your grade in the class?"

"It just dropped to an eighty-nine!" Her eyes got wide, "An eighty- freaking -nine, Axel, so close to an 'A', yet so far,"

"Are you kidding me, I wish I had at least a 'D' in any of my classes,"

"You could absolutely have all 'A's if you wanted to, Axel, but how are you going to be passing classes that you don't even show up to?" She slowly lets a smile make its way to her face.

That's what I've been looking for, that was the goal of the conversation.

"There's that smile," I cooed, "Stop studying, if you're gonna fail it, you're gonna fail it,"

She shoots me an annoyed glance,

"Wow thanks, how helpful."

"I try, I try,"

She shakes her head looking out of the window for a moment. "Is there something you need?"

"Just spending time with my favorite person,"

Again, she shoots me a pointed look.

"What? Am I not your favorite person too?"

"No, Noah is," She tries hard to hide her cheeky smile.

"Tread lightly, angel, you might make me jealous,"

"You being jealous sounds like a personal issue."

Always so quick-witted, always having a response. This is Victoria Beckette everyone - never to be outwitted.

"You think you're so funny," I tease.

"I'm the funniest person I know, babe,"

"I like it when you call me that," I coo, "Say it again,"

She sighs loudly, letting her head fall back to the window. "How are you so annoying at seven in the morning,"

"I think you bring it out of me."

I smile as she starts to gather her things. She may try to hide it but I can see that cute smile that she tries to hide.

"And where are you going?" I quip amused.

She turns to me; lips pursed, book in hand, hand on hip. "To go beat up some more of your bitches-"

"-Now leave me alone."

Chapter 26

The week went one tormentingly slow; most likely because I was looking forward to the party Friday. I let it slip to Mia, but I emitted some details - like the fact that I was going with Axel Stone.

Why? It was our little secret.

Hundreds of rumors surround Axel, all of them bad. Still, I don't see the troublemaker they talk about when I'm with him. Annoying? Yes. Stupid? Yes. Undeniably attractive? Yes. A malicious criminal that wreaks havoc for personal gain? Absolutely not.

Tonight, I'm going to feel free again. I'm going to let go of what I have to be and do only what I want. If only for a few hours, I would still be content at the end of the day.

I wanted to misbehave tonight and make up for it tomorrow morning

"Don't get too drunk, remember we're going shopping in the morning," Mia laughs walking me to my car.

"Are you sure you don't want to make an appearance?" I plead one last time, already knowing the answer.

"After Liv stopped tutoring me in German I have to take nights like this to study," She sighs dramatically.

I would've offered to help her with German if I wasn't almost a hundred percent sure I would only make it worse.

"You do you, pretty lady, I'll text you after the party." I blow her a kiss and pull out of the student parking lot.

I let the windows down, music blasting through the speakers of my car, on my way home. The wind blew my hair wild. I take the time to appreciate the outside world; my life at home isn't so serene.

I wonder if being poor with a happy family would be better than a rich, broken home. My thoughts would sound selfish out of context - hell maybe they sound selfish in context. I do believe that money can make a person happier. However, this isn't my money. I am not the one that's rich.

With that being said, I still have it overwhelmingly good. I eat and I sleep under a roof - basic human necessities. Nevertheless, no matter how hard I try, I can't ignore the fact that the only thing that fills my home is the heat of hatred. Hatred of everyone that lives within the home, as well as outside of the home. Tenison holds up the walls. Resentment pads the floor.

The only common ground within that house is that everyone is unhappy, for different reasons, but still unhappy.

How could I - a rich girl with every American's teenage dream - think about another life?

Am I crazy?

Am I unappreciative?

Am I selfish?

Yes. I am all of those things and I'm about to be a terrible daughter. Maybe I am ungrateful, in all actuality, I probably am. Be as that may, I deserve to be happy - rich or poor.

I slam my car door, excitement pulsating through my veins. I had about five hours to get ready. Honestly dreading that I told Axel to pick me up at ten instead of eight. It sounded like a good line at the time, but now all I wanted to do was be under strobing lights dancing wildly.

I open the door to my home instantly taking note of the angry voices coming from the kitchen.

"We haven't even walked down the aisle and you're cheating on me!"

"Know your place, woman! Where do you get off talking to me like that?"

"You promised me that we would be different! You said you wouldn't treat me like the others."

"I lied." A loud sound breaks up the words. "Get over it."

I continue up the stairs. Minding your business is always the better option, I would only make things worse. From the few lines I could pick up it's obvious what the argument about. They have been fighting back and forth for several days about the same reporter; maybe a few other women, it's hard to tell.

Clearly, my father is insatiable and nothing is ever enough. However, I can't have complete sympathy for the woman because this is the exact way she got him - through an affair. It's clear that there would be more fights after the wedding. Again, all I have to do is wait until I turn eighteen. Then, these fights will be nothing but a past obstacle.

Hell, at least it wasn't me who he was arguing with

<3

It took all five hours to get into my bad bitch headspace, but once I was in it I was ready to take on the world. I looked great and I felt even better. All I was waiting for was a call from the devil.

The loving sound of my ringtone cuts through the music I was playing on my phone.

Speak of the devil and he shall appear

"Hello?"

"You ready?"

"I was born ready,"

"Shut up, I'm outside."

I smile into the phone, grabbing everything I need, and fly down the stairs. I almost made it to the door scot-free. All the lights were off except one, of course, the kitchen. With the kitchen light comes a person still awake,

"Victoria,"

We've been through this too many times. I could only guess that he was extra annoyed seeing me after his argument with his mistress earlier.

"Yes, Father?"

"What did I tell you about going out with that boy?"

"What boy?"

"That, Stone, boy." My father rears the corner, scowl very present on his face.

"What the hell are you wearing?" His voice booms in the foyer.

"I won't get caught. I'm sure there aren't any paparazzi at a high school party," I suppress an eye-roll. "I'll be back before morning,"

"Victoria, I swear to the heavens if you don't get your ungrateful ass back in this house-"

The door slams, my father on one side and me on the other. I stare at it, not being able to believe I just did that. I quickly run down the stairs into Axel's dark car. I was glad he didn't bring the motorcycle, I didn't want to flash everyone on the highway. Axel probably figured that as well.

I let out a breath as I slide into the passenger seat. Axel looking at me with a slight smile.

"Father."

We say at the same time, I laugh shaking my head.

"It's okay," I smile over at him, "Now let's go!"

"You look good," He gives me a once over before pull out of my driveway.

"You look better," I retort with a teasing smile, his eyes gleam in surprise before he replaces it with amusement.

"I'll have to steal that one,"

"It's all yours."

That was it, the night air filled the comfortable silence, and music eased my nerves. We didn't have to talk in the presence of one another. If there was nothing to say, let it be. This was the time to relax before being thrown into a crazed party.

A smile rested on my face, I couldn't wipe it off even if I wanted to.

The thought crossed my mind that this is the place where I want to be. Careless, in the passenger seat of a hot car. My father and his mistress faded, my mother and her addiction were not on my conscience.

"I like you better like this," Axel praised while pulling off of the interstate.

"Me too."

From the car, I could hear the music of the party, my excitement reels back up. Teens littered the yard, talking, and drinking. Cars were lined from the house to the top of the neighborhood. I can't remember whose party this is, but I only know a few people that can pack a party like this.

Axel guides me in through a side door by the small of my back. His touch leaves warm radiating from my back up to my cheeks. I do my best to cool my flaming face.

It wasn't long we were walking through the maze of people until we found the group. All of them sat on a couch in the corner of the living room. They look just as cool as they always did. The aura that radiated off of them was not one I could define, I just knew I wanted to be a part of it.

"Victoria, you're going to give me a heart attack!" Athena was the first one to notice our presence. A smile is instantly on my face.

"Nothing could compare you, babe," I smile back at her, moving my gaze to the rest of the couch.

"What's up, Tori?"

"You look pretty, Victoria."

"Damn, girl."

I give Tyler a pointed look for his comment, smiling at Noah and rolling my eyes at Kaiden. Axel's arm moves up to my shoulder as he settles on a wall next to the couch.

"Is Blaze here?"

"Yup, and Scarlette,"

"The redhead?" Athena nods, "This night just got one hundred times better!"

The conversation is effortless as we all hang out around the couch. Axel's arm was still on my shoulders, but I had moved to sit on the couch's arm. Despite the loud music, we were able to talk and laugh without a problem.

"I'm going to go get a drink, sit here and look pretty," Axel whispers in my ear and his weight is lifted from my body.

Yeah -fucking- right

I look over at Athena, "That dance floor looks like it needs something." I tease with a smile.

"Yeah, some bad bitches."

***

< Outfit Described (Front and Back) >

Chapter 27

It's like she read my mind, taking me by the arm and leading me to the middle of the living that was doubling as the dance floor for the time being. It did its job; two loudspeakers sat in the corner of the room and they shook the entire house.

Music blasted out of the speakers at a deafening volume. Not only could you hear the music, but you could also feel it course through you. It vibrated my entire being with familiar music. Music so loud it made my teeth chatter.

Slow to fast, up and down - no set genre to the music whatsoever.

I couldn't tell you exactly what I was doing, but I knew I felt great. The songs flowed through me, then add the energy of the girls. This was a drug within itself. Both Blaze and Scarlette joined our personal dance circle not too long after it was created.

Four

Five

Six

Songs pass, but the natural high still hadn't left.

I need a drink

People around us were loud with encouraging yells, probably on a real high. Whether it was at us, or just in general. I didn't know or care.

"What do they have in the kitchen?" I ask pushing through the maze of people.

"I think they have some Hennessy, but what are you into?"

"Did you say, Hennessy?" Scarlette pipes in with a smile.

I didn't want alcohol, Mia and I had something to do tomorrow. Maybe I could invite these girls. Our old friend group had completely turned on her after what she told me. I knew these girls would accept her just as they did me. Who knows? Maybe one of them knows some German.

I search the fridge for a sealed bottle of water and shift my attention back to the girls.

"We've never had this much fun until you started going to parties," Blaze smiled brightly over at me, "I designate you as our hype girl,"

I laugh.

"I agree, we've never had a dance circle formed before." Athena drinks straight out of the Hennessy bottle before passing it to Scarlette.

"I didn't even notice the circle," I breathe heavily.

"Want to know who did notice?" Athena edges, "A certain bad boy."

I suppress my smile in front of the girls, taking a sip of my water to hide the giddiness of my heart. I had an itch to start something. The fire brewed in the pit of my stomach begging me to act on the thoughts I was currently having.

"Pass the Hennessy,"

I only took a gulp, enough to feel the liquid burn my chest. I just wanted to add some lighter fluid to the already burning fire. Something to spark my confidence.

"I'll be back."

I don't even look twice at the heavily smiling group of girls. I had one thing on my mind and one thing only: Find Axel.

Entering the living room again, I scan the room finding Axel still sitting on the couch. Beer in hand and grey eyes scanning the room as well. The Hennessy's burn certainly did what I wanted to. I didn't even have time to think before my legs were moving in his direction. The sound of my heels against the wood floor mixed with the slow playing music just encouraged me.

"How'd you like my dance?" I whispered in his ear, "I heard you were watching,"

"It was mesmerizing, angel, "

"I could give you a private one," His head raises to mine, surprised by my rather valiant behavior.

I absolutely love his eyes

"Victoria," He warned.

"Come dance with me." I pull him towards the music, yet he doesn't budge.

"I don't dance,"

"I don't care."

I tug once more, but Axel counters my actions by pulling me down onto him. The boys came back from where ever they'd been and paused. Axel shot them a look and they got the message. Soon turning on their heels walking back to where they came from.

"You look stunning tonight," His hands rest on my waist, nose snuggled into my neck.

I was hot, I felt hot from my face to my feet. His touch, the Hennessy, this room packed with sweating, dancing teenagers.

"Come outside with me," I get up from his lap. "It's getting hot in here,"

"Yeah, it's me." He laughs but gets up anyway.

The cold night air is instantly refreshing. It was clear with absolutely no stars, but the moon was full enough to light the sky. The only sound out here was the humming music inside of the house, you could still feel the thumping of the music.

We were silent.

Again, just bathing in the presence of one another. The burn in my chest was gone as well as my firey confidence. Axel stood next to me on the porch, looking into the dark night sky. The faint smell of weed was a humorous reminder of where we are.

I let my gaze fall on Axel, he was paying me no mind while watching a bird pass. I took note of the bird, knowing exactly what it was.

He was heart throbbingly gorgeous, Axel, not the bird-

"Let's get out of here," Axel states after a moment of silence. I smile.

"Where to?"

"Anywhere with a road,"

With a smile and pull of the arm, we made our way to his car. The thrill of an adventure was heavy on my heart. I had gone driving during a dark night before, but doing with Axel made it special for me. I would most likely never admit how much these small spontaneous adventures with him meant to me. I wouldn't need to. I was happy for the time being. Nothing mattered but me, him, and the moon.

The car sped through an empty highway. I hadn't even the smallest clue of what time it was. I didn't have an urge to check.

It's the promise of life that makes the darkness so appealing. I'd read a quote like that once. I didn't understand the meaning of it at the time, because I'd never been in a position to understand it. It applies now. It was now that I understand the beauty of that quote.

I let down my window, sticking my head out of it. The time I had spent on the curls in my hair flew out with it. Material things didn't matter. I didn't care about time or money, things or people.

Somehow, I felt as if I had been longing for this. How could that be? I had never experienced this before yet my heart yearned for it. My heart yearns for something I cannot understand.

It feels like an imaginary tug. I want to release it but I don't know how. So many passions lie within me that I have yet to explore. I have so much potental; if I would just get my life together - imagine what I could do.

Imagine who I could be.

Imagine who I could be with.

"That's a bad idea, doll," Axel laughs from next to me. Gesturing to my entire head being stuck out of the window.

I smile, "We were out of good ideas a long time ago."

I do, however, pull my head back in. Still leaving the window down, I turn to Axel. I'm sure my hair was as wild as the smile on my face. Axel just looks at me, a smile settling on his lips. We were staring at each other in pure euphoria.

Then, as if on cue, we both just laugh.

Laughing until our stomachs hurt.

Laughing until there are tears in our eyes.

Laughing so hard that Axel pulls the car over on the side of the highway so we don't crash.

Then after that, we laugh even harder.

It was him,

He was where the tug was leading to

~ Chapter 28 ~

L ast night was the first time I'd snuck into my own home.

When I come home late, normally I would just go through the front door and try to be quiet. I have snuck out before, but never in.

I'm not dense.

I remember very well how I left my home before the party. Running into my father while coming back was not something I wanted to experience. My father wasn't one to let time settle his fury.

If he was home this morning, I would have to sneak out of the house to go to the mall. However, both he and his mistress happen to be out of the house.

As soon as I woke up this morning I texted Athena. I asked if she and the girls wanted to join us at the mall. Of course, not without asking Mia if she was okay with it. She'd been even more excited to meet them than I was.

I settled into a parking spot at the mall, trying to slow my breathing. The very thought of my father got my heart rate up. I didn't want to hang out with the girls with a bad vibe. They didn't deserve that.

I hop out of my car with a fake plastered smile. When I get in the mall, maybe the smile won't be so fake anymore.

I was correct, as soon as I spot Athena a real smile appears on my face.

"Aren't you hungover?" I tease walking up to the table they occupied. Mia still wasn't there.

"High tolerance, baby," She winks, hugging me.

"Is that the case for all of you?"

"Redheads can take their liquor, it's a fact,"

"People named Blaze are automatically superior."

I can't argue with that.

We fall into a comfortable conversation, waiting for Mia. Apparently, after I disappeared last night the party ended up being broken up by the police. I can only imagine what kind of things I would have to go through if I came home in a cop car. I don't think I'd be living right now.

My phone buzzes in my pocket:

"Hello?"

"Okay, I'm here!"

I could hear the excitement in Mia's voice as she squeals breathlessly into the phone.

"Come on in, we're waiting for you."

Seconds later the bright-eyed brunette walks through the doors. Eyes searching the crowded area wildly. I wave my hand trying to get her attention, immediately her eyes land on me.

"Is that her? She's so pretty!" Athena greets her before I do with an open hug. I smile at the two.

"Mia, this is Athena,"

"That-" I gesture at Blaze. "Raven-haired cutie is Blaze,"

Blaze winks at me in return, "Any friend of Victoria, is a friend of mine,"

"And you've already met Scarlette,"

Scarlette blows a kiss.

"Well, now that introductions are made. Let's start shopping!"

"You don't have to tell me twice-"

<3

Five whole hours later, we'd finally finished. It was very eventful though. I absolutely love to online shop from my cozy bed, but something about buying clothes from the mall just hits different.

There's something authentic about it

As soon as I wave goodbye to the girls and get situated in my car. Every worry that I had pushed away to have fun with them, came back in a suffocating wave. It just now dawned on me that my father might have a problem with how much I spent today.

Yes, I worked and got some money, but I'd always been accustomed to picking up his card and going. I really am dependent on him...

No matter how much I try to work and get away from him, something is always tied back to him. It's incredibly infuriating. I'm constantly running in circles. I'm stuck.

Déjà vu

The mall is definitely way too close to my house. I quickly grab my bags and try to walk through the front door as quiet as a mouse. I absolutely did not look over the extra car in the drive.

Daddy's home

I made it to my room, not as much as a creak came from anywhere in the house. As soon as my door shut, however, my heart was back to beating rapidly.

"Victoria,"

The voice of my father was loud, but not angry. That is what scared me even more.

I set whatever bags I had in my arms down and immediately went downstairs. My father was sitting at the island behind a glass of whiskey, again.

"Yes?"

His eyes blazed up towards me, I was the object of his anger at this moment.

"Not only did you go out to some heathenous party, but you also went out and spent three hundred dollars worth of clothes at the mall!" His voice bounced off the kitchen walls as they normally did.

"Have you lost your goddamn mind?" His teeth grip the whiskey glass as he takes a sip.

"I'll pay you ba-"

"Yes! With the fucking job you got! At the very place, I'm trying to get rid of!" He screams at me again.

"I mean really, can you do anything right?" He seethes into his whiskey glass. Tears build up in my eyes. I normally can shake him off, but today, his words actually get me.

"I told you I was going to get a job,"

"I expect you to have a little bit of sense, child. I'm not going to put up with this shit all my life. If you think I'm bluffing about kicking you out as soon as you turn eighteen, you're mistaken,"

"You kicking me out of this house will be the best thing to ever happen to me!" I snapped, I can't recall how many times I've yelled at my father in my lifetime, but I know all times have not gone very well.

He slams his glass back on the island, "Watch your fucking tone, Victoria!"

His fists are balled and he's no longer behind the island. I get a quick flashback of the moment on the stairs. Tears instantly gush out of my eyes.

"Please hit me again!" I scream, "I will shut all this shit down, I will go to the police, to the news, you will never get to be Mayor! Hit me a- fucking -gain!"

He pauses in his spot, nose literally flaring in fury.

"You think I like hating you?" My voice was calmer now.

"Every day I have to be your punching bag, I have to listen to every reason why I'm not good enough," I continue, seeing that I have his attention.

"I'm sorry. I'm sorry for spending that money today, I was wrong. I'm sorry for getting the job, but it didn't have anything to do with you. I will not quit it,"

"Even with my apology you still won't love me!"

It slipped, I didn't mean to go that far with him. His look did not change and it broke my heart for the millionth time. So it's true...

"I mean, I really do try to make your life easier, but nothing is ever good enough. I'm going to graduate valedictorian and early! I lie beautifully in front of the cameras when prompted. In public, I always paint you in an amazing light!" I'm sure I looked crazy, this is the first time in all my life I have ever stood up to my father.

"I'm sorry, I'm sorry, I'm sorry-" He mocks me in a high voice, "Those are the only words you ad your worthless mother know!"

I'm stunned into silence, I can barely see a clear outline of him through blurred tears.

"I am surrounded by useless people! I can never catch a break! Just stop fucking shit up. I don't give a shit about your apology, I don't give a shit about you!" He seethes with so much rage I can feel his spit fall onto my cheek. I don't dare wipe it off though.

"Don't you ever forget your place! You are to follow my instructions entirely, you have no choice. That is your role, that is your only role." He not even yelling anymore.

"I'm not even asking for love. I'm asking to not feel afraid in my own home," I swallow, keeping my eyes glued to the floor. With such a hateful speech like he just gave me, it would be pathetic to back down now.

I am not useless

"So I'm the bad guy now, huh?"

I sigh, "You'll never change, but at least I know that now."

With that, I turn and went up the stairs. My head felt like it was swimming. I can't even comprehend the fact that my father just called me useless. The little girl in me begged desperately for him to call after me. If he did, I would have jumped into his arms as I've always wanted to do. All he has to do is tell me he didn't mean. That work is getting to him. That he'd work on his anger.

Silence. He doesn't call after me. I, instead, hear the shatter of his glass in the kitchen.

I slam my door, sliding my back down it. I let everything out. I didn't muffle my cries. If someone heard them, they would simply turn away.

I'm so stupid, what did I think was going to come out of that conversation? Did I really think he was going to instantly drop whatever hatred had built over the years because I cried to him?

I'm stupid

So, so, stupid.

Chapter 29

Three thirty-five a.m.

My back is still pressed against my door. My limbs are still shaking and I haven't been able to stop crying since I hit the ground. The ruckus downstairs gave me the slightest bit in comfort. Hearing the multiple things crash downstairs my father felt something.

I had gotten to him, maybe not the way I wanted to, but he feels something.

I don't know what an anxiety attack feels like, but I feel like this is pretty close. I would search up my symptoms but my phone is in my bag across the room and I don't feel like I can move.

What's an anxiety attack?

What's a panic attack?

Are they different? Shut up, of course, they are.

Why am I having chest pains?

Am I going to die? No, I'm not going to die.

Jesus Christ, I really am my worst enemy. My heart rate is what's scaring me. I could feel it in my throat when I first came upstairs, but now that it's been several hours I know it's not from the lack of exercise. The heaving of my chest just gets harder.

Whatever this is it will end. Panic attacks or anxiety attacks- whatever the fuck. It always ends. I haven't been here before, but I will get out just fine.

I will live

I'm fine

I will live

I'm fine

This will end

I'm fine-

I continue to chant to myself, slowly rocking side to side. If only I could lull myself to sleep. I'll figure everything out later, but right now, I need to sleep. The floor is going to have to do because moving to the bed seems like an impossible task at this moment.

Everything will be alright in the morning-

<3

The slam of the door woke me up.

I was on the floor, where I'd last remembered. My body no longer trembling, my heart at a normal pace. I could already feel the swelling of my eyes as I tried to adjust to the light in the room.

I moved slowly to the windows of my balcony, seeing the driveway empty except for my car. I'd overheard one of my father's conversations last week.

He and his mistress would be going to the final meeting with the wedding planner today. I check the time-

Eleven forty-six a.m.

A thought caressed my mind, but as soon as I could fully grasp it, it was gone. The itch to do what it said grew.

My mother

What rehab is she at? My father must know. He probably looked it up. He probably looked it up and didn't delete his history...

I snuck downstairs to my dad's home office. He only occupies two rooms when he's home: The kitchen and his office.

It used to be three: His bedroom. However, since his mistress has moved in with us. She's normally in there and he's in the office drinking.

Creaking the door open, I slip in. It was dark in wood and green velvet-covered every sitting surface in there. It smelled like the library - wonderful. I shake my head, that's not why I'm in here.

I move to his computer. The sign-in pop up made my heart drop. I have no idea what his password is.

I try his birthday: 09/26/78 - Wrong

I look around the room for a clue. If it's his mistress's birthday then I'm shit out of luck because I wouldn't even know how to start looking for that. Half of the time I can't even remember her name. It wouldn't be my mother's, but I tried it - Wrong.

I don't know anyone that my father cares about. He wasn't the closest with his parents. Thinking about it, I really don't know much about my father or about my parents in general. My fingers pause at the keys in realization.

Suddenly the last sixteen years of my life are a blur.

I can't remember previous conversations that I've had with my parents, yet I know I've had them. I can't remember my grandparents' faces, yet I know I've seen them. I can't remember when I learned how to ride a bike or if I ever did learn.

I don't know how to ride a bike - I've never had a bike.

I shake my head again, that's not why I'm here.

I try one last thing, my birthday: 02/18/04 - Correct

The computer opens to the desktop. I just stare at it. He screams and cusses at me, just to go into his office and have me as his password? I would love to think this was because he wanted to put it like that. However, I knew my father a little better than that. Nothing he did was genuine. He only does good things for bragging rights.

I go into his history, scrolling by the few questionable things in there and going to the day he told me about the phone call. I was looking for anything with the words rehabilitation. It wasn't long before I found a website that said: Morris Village Alcohol and Drug Treatment Center reviews.

That's definitely where she is

Before closing out of the history tab, I saw right under that website was another one. This website seemed to be a google search: How to make a divorce private? For some reason, I just don't think that was for my mother.

But I'll mind my business

I check out all of his tabs and close the computer. Making sure everything in his office is exactly the way I found it. I grab my keys for the kitchen counter and head for my car.

Time to see mommy

<3

"Hello, how can I help you?" A woman with a sickly sweet southern accent asks me as soon as I enter the door. After the hour and a half drive, it was nice to hear.

"Yes, I believe my mother is enrolled here," I really didn't know if she was here. This could have been a total waste of time, but it's not like I had anything better to do. If she wasn't here I would just go get a burger or something and go home.

"Oh, great! What's your mother's name?" The woman smiles brightly at me as she shifts around her desk.

"Jessica Beckette."

The woman's eyes look back up at me sharply. She then lets out a small sigh.

"Yes, she's new," She states pressing her lips together. "She's also not ad-justing well. Normally with patients like that, we don't let them have any contact with the outside world. In case, something was to trigger them to do something not so good,"

"Oh, okay-"

"But, maybe, in this case, seeing you will help her situation. That and I would feel terrible having to send you back after you've come here to see your mother." Her bright smile returns to her face as she escorts me through a long hallway.

Why can't I have parents like this?

"Do you have any kids-" I look at her name tag, "Ms. Jones?"

"Yes ma'am, and I hope if I was in this situation they'd come to see me as you've made the effort to do,"

Imagine having a normal mother - I wonder what that feels like

Ms. Jones stops me in front of a baby blue door. It looked dull compared to the other doors, despite its bright color. I smile back at Ms. Jones. Pressing against the handle of the door as I hear her heels click away from me.

A thin dark-haired woman sits on her bed gazing out of the window. A bottle of wine pressed to her lips. Pieces of glass litter the floor of her bedroom and the blankets have been torn from her flimsy twin bed.

Her head doesn't even shift at the sound of the door opening.

"Hi, mom."

~ Chapter 30 ~

W hy am I here?

As soon as I saw the state she was in. I could no longer remember. Did I want her to comfort me? Did I just want to lay eyes on her? What could we talk about except the obvious?

She was in rehab, yet still drinking as if she was home.

The sound of my voice made her turn around. Glass bottle still pressed to her lips. Even the sight of me wouldn't make her drop it. As soon as she looked at me her eyes were back on the window. My stomach started to bubble, I no longer wanted to be here.

"When I told you to take care of yourself, this isn't what I meant." It was meant to come out as a joke, but the air around the sentence was dead.

It hung - it was acknowledged, but not spoken upon.

"I came all this way and I still can't get even a hello from you?" I kept all my things on me. I don't plan on staying long.

"What? Was the mansion getting too big for you? You had to leave and see your poor mother?"

I was used to the cruel words from my father. However, my mother had never spoken to me this way. I knew it was part of her being drunk, but what did she want from me? We had this conversation the day she moved out. She knows better than anyone why I'm staying with my dad. I don't even know why she would bring it up.

"Like I have a choice-"

"Right, because the mansion is the lesser option," She retorts right back, still not facing me.

"Even if leaving was an option - Where else could I go? With you? In this rehab facility?" I snap, "Don't forget that mansion used to be your home too,"

"I could never forget,"

I was a little confused about where all this animosity was coming from. For the life of me, I can't understand why she could be so angry, well, so angry at me. I try desperately to remember a happier time. A time when my family was all together, laughing or smiling. All I came up with was a blank. It's just like earlier this morning in my father's office.

Why can't I remember my childhood?

"Is that all?" I whisper after a moment of silence.

She glances at me from the corner of her eye. The bottle in her hand falters. There's another crisp moment of silence before I just decide for her.

Opening the door without a word and I walk out. Feeling tears in my eyes, but trying to blink them back. I wouldn't even say I'm sad.

I'm fed up.

I don't know why people feel like they can treat me like shit, but I won't allow it anymore. I'm finishing what I have to finish so I get out of my situation. I deserve better than this. I know I do.

I smile at Ms. Jones as I pass her. Getting into my car and driving off. An hour and a half drive for a five-minute conversation with the one person I came to see. I wanted her to see me drive off. Through that tiny window of hers, I wanted her to realize where she is and what she's done to herself. The brute conversations with my parents should make it easier to cut them off. In reality, it's just not that easy for so many different reasons.

I let my car blaze on the nearly empty highway. I don't want to go home right now, but where else could I go?

I got an idea, picking up my phone. It rings twice before it picks up:

"Hi, babe!" Athena's voice rings in my ears.

"What are you doing, Green-eyes?"

"Waiting for you to make my life better. I'll send you the address,"

"Great."

<3

"The entertainment has arrived!" Athena sings as she walks me into the back room of the racing track.

When I saw the place they were at I was sort of apprehensive. Most of the time I don't intentionally make my father angry. I laid some ground rules for myself: I wouldn't stay until dark and I would stay away from any cameras.

"How are you, love?" I kiss Blaze and Scarlette on the cheek. Sitting on the arm of the couch they sat.

"You didn't ask me how I was doing," Tyler winks over at me, a jab to the chest comes from Axel.

"You guys just hang out around here?"

"We were practicing, but then we got hungry," Noah - my favorite - smiles at me, which I return.

I remember Axel's bike. It's been a while since I've been on it. I'm getting withdrawal symptoms. These thoughts lead my gaze to Axel. He was sitting on the couch across from me, eyes glued to his phone. The only reason I could even tell that he knew I was here was him hitting Tyler for his comment. I pull out my phone to match his energy:

Hi to you too

I engage in a conversation with everybody else in the room. I can see his reaction when he gets my text, I can see him smirk from my peripheral vision. My phone vibrates on my lap:

Sorry, Angel, I know how much you love my attention

Can't live without it ;)

I decide to play even harder. Turning my phone face down on my lap and becoming truly involved in the conversation. When feeling my phone goes off I turn it over, look at it, then continue what I was saying - not giving Axel a response. My phone continued to go off:

What are you going to do about it then?

Oh, so you're not going to respond?

Dangerous game you're playing, lovely.

Just know that I'm the best at it.

"Where's the bathroom, Athena?" I ask standing up, surpassing a smile as I feel Axel's eyes on me.

"On the rig-"

"I'll show her."

Axel cuts Athena off walking behind me, leading me out of the door.

"I think I'm good-"

"Wouldn't want you getting lost, Princess."

He leads me by the small of my back, and for some reason, I don't think we're going to the bathroom. That's okay because I don't actually have to use it. We make it to the parking lot before he finally lets go of his hold on my waist.

"I don't think this is the bathroom." I smile slyly, leaning against some old wooden fence.

"Oops, I must've taken a wrong turn," Axel was close, I could feel his breath on my face. The familiar smell of wood, mint, and menthol flood my nose.

"Then what are we still doing out here?" My voice was barely above a whisper. It didn't need to be any louder, I'm sure at this proximity he could hear the rapid beating of my heart.

There was a thick silence between us. It was thick because we both wanted to do something, but neither of us would make the move to do it. I'm not a mind reader, I don't know if what he wants and what I want are the same thing. However, the embarrassment of me making a move that he doesn't want is enough to keep my body in place.

"Will you teach me how to ride?"

He chokes, "T- Teach you how to ride what?"

"Your bike," I tilt my head. I'm really going to need him to stop choking because I didn't pay attention in P.E. when they taught us CPR.

His face is washed with a pink color and he backs away slightly. I can't help but wonder if I said something wrong. Yes, I changed the subject, but did I ruin it?

"What do you want with a bike?" Axel recovers pulling a cigarette out of his jacket pocket.

"The same thing you want with a bike," I retort, "Don't you ride for the feeling? The wind blowing through your hair,"

His eyes lock with mine. "You ride for the ease of mind, right? There's something dangerous about driving on two wheels at hundred-thirty miles per hour. You love it and I want to love it too."

I was gazing at him now, truly seeing him for the first time. I was seeing Axel in all his glory: Smoking, leaning on his bike, and full attention on me.

This was Axel Stone ladies and gentlemen

"Hop on."

Chapter 31

The beautiful bike purred under me. Riding her on the dirt track seemed unfair. Machinery of this craftsmanship belongs on a long paved highway, with no other object but itself.

I was grinning from ear to ear. I was looking at the track ahead and all the bumps were daunting. Axel insisted I start off on an easier track but my ego wouldn't allow it. I blink towards Axel. His hands gripping at the fence, eyebrows furrowed. He nods at me, giving me the go-ahead to move.

I adjusted the tight helmet on my head, then - I was off.

The air caressed my face as I slowly made my way down one of the hills. Sheer terror was the only thing holding me back. It feels like I have no control but all the control in the world at the same time.

I feel vulnerable; I can and will die if I crash this bike.

I feel blessed; I can feel all the elements against my skin.

Starting to get my nerve back up I rotated my wrist on the throttle. The wind whipping my neck harder than before. My shirt begging to fly off with the wind. I was flying, soaring through the track.

I was on a high, however, internally calm and at peace.

The few people around the track became colorful blurs. Trees looked like blobs of green and the dirt under me started to look like the road to heaven - in both ways.

My throat is dry from my large open-mouthed smile. How have I never experienced this? I pity anyone that hasn't felt the joy and freedom of riding.

The beauty growls from under me again, picking up the speed. She hums almost as if she's alive. I think that's what makes me trust her. I feel dangerously sexy. Like once I get off the bike I'm going to remove my helmet and shake my hair like the girls in the movies.

I let go of the throttle completely, trying to slow down. I saw the large hill coming up and I decided that I wasn't going to challenge it. Unfortunately, the bike slowed but not at the rate I needed it to.

Ecstasy turned into terror as I strained my neck to find Axel. He's already on the track. He was talking to me, but I couldn't hear him over the engine. The last thing I wanted to do was harm his bike. Especially after I had begged him to teach me to ride. I knew that going full send on the brakes would just harm both me and the bike.

I had to think; Treat it like a car

I eased on the brake, the bike slowed. I turned the handles letting the side of the bike face the large hill in an attempt to create more friction. The dirt kicked up and the wheels froze. Chuckling at myself, I get off the bike.

Arms wrap around me as I trip on the space from the ground and the bike. Axel catches me in his arms and the bike with his foot.

I reach my arms around his neck, "That was amazing!"

"I'm glad you liked it, princess, but you nearly gave me a heart attack,"

"Thank you for catching me," I smile as he places me back down, going to tend to his bike.

"I'll always catch you."

He stated it nonchalantly, wheeling his bike back to the parking lot. The little jump my heart did blanked my mind. I had no words - utterly speechless. What's even more infuriating is that I'm pretty sure he said that cheesy line on purpose because he's a narcissistic asshole, but he's a cute narcissistic asshole so it still had an effect.

"Do you ever thinking about just riding away?" I changed the subject.

He turned to me, "What do you mean?"

"Like when you're riding, you get this sense of freedom. I would think it gets hard to not take random road trips,"

"Trust me, I take random road trips all the time," He chuckles, "That's the main reason I don't show up to school,"

Oops, I forgot he needs to go to court for truancy

"That was almost alright, Tori," Kaiden yells from the other side of the fence. He was decked out in racing gear, helmet in hand. That dumb smirk lacing his face.

"That was almost a compliment Kaiden," He shrugs hopping over the fence to join us.

"Are you going to the race Wednesday?"

"No,"

They televise those events, so even though I would love to see Axel race in person I'm going to have to settle with watching it on TV.

"Why? Afraid daddy might see you?" He chuckles to himself.

I hit him in the gut causing him to crouch over spuing a slur of colorful words. Axel snorts from next to me.

"I'm really trying to like you, Kaiden, but you just keep talking."

<3

"What made you want to be my date?"

Lucas was standing over where I sat in the Library. Ms. Boucher stated that she wanted us to pick a French book out of the library and write a report on it. Honestly, I think she's just run out of ideas. I'm not complaining though. I'd rather read a book I can't understand than listen to her teaching.

I furrow my brows, "I'm sorry?"

"My father told me that we'd be attending the wedding together. He said that Mr. Beckette insisted you wanted it,"

That son of a bitch-

"Oh yeah, sorry you just caught me off guard," I shift on the bench so Lucas could sit down, "I remember you telling me that you weren't really into that type of crowd. I don't really like weddings, so we can be miserable together," A mayor's daughter has to be good at lying, right?

"You beat me to it, I had planned on asking you," He chuckles pulling out his choice of novel.

The Plague - interesting.

I return my gaze back to my book. I decided on The Lover by Marguerite Duras. They had the French copy and the English copy, I had both. The French copy in my bookbag and the English copy currently in my lap.

"The Lover?" Lucas scoffs, "Sounds dumb,"

"You're dumb,"

"You don't have to be rude."

I laugh quietly. His accent only made the sentence funnier. I set my book down, getting the clue that he wanted to continue a conversation.

"Do you remember when the reports du-"

I'm cut off by the slam of the library doors. In walks, all four idiots, looking smug as ever. Axel made it a point to look between Lucas and me, then sit across the room. I looked out of the window next to me. At the ground level, his motorcycle was parked alongside some other sleek-looking cars.

He must have seen us when he pulled up

Why do I feel guilty? We're not dating. If he's upset about me sitting with Lucas I wonder how he'll feel about me suddenly going to my father's wedding with him as my date.

"What color is your dress for Friday? I might as well match you,"

"Friday?"

"That is when the wedding takes place, isn't it?"

"Yup," Oh my God, is it really this Friday? "White,"

"The same as the bride?"

"Yes, it was my father's idea. Something about looking like a unit, he says a family that styles together stays together."

He didn't say that - However, he did tell me to wear white. It's to be vindictive against his mistress, but I will do what he asked of me.

"You're staring,"

Lucas's words caused me to blink towards him. I was shocked for multiple reasons. One of them being that I didn't even notice I was staring at Axel. The second being I wouldn't think that Lucas would've noticed. I didn't intentionally look at Axel. I was thinking and my gaze drifted.

"I'm not," I reply, "I was staring in his direction, not at him,"

"Then why did you have that look on your face?"

"What are you talking about?" I ask, "What look?"

"You looked at him about you looked at the stars that one night on the balcony, at the dinner," He explains, "You look at him like you looked at the stars,"

"And?"

"You love the stars, remember?"

"After three conversations with me, you think you know me, huh?" I hmphed, putting on a light smile so he would see I wasn't upset with him.

"I'm observant,"

"Is that what you call it?" I locked eyes with Axel one last time before turning my head with a smile towards Lucas.

"So white tie?"

"White tie."

<h1 style="text-align:center">~ Chapter 32 ~</h1>

F riday's wedding was a whole affair. Although, I wouldn't expect anything less from my father. I woke up to makeup artists knocking at my bedroom door. They got me into the dress I picked and styled me, all that took three hours.

Then I was driven to the place where the wedding would be held. It was gorgeous without a doubt. Very formal and expensive looking. I could see the red carpet that the soon-to-be-married couple would walk down.

I've been thrown around all day; whether someone wants a blurb on how I feel or an assistant of my father telling me last-minute changes he's made - I've had something to do for every minute today.

I'm finally standing still for the first time, at the door. I was smiling and talking to any guest that entered the wedding doors. Some I recognized, others I had no idea of.

The first guests to arrive were paparazzi and reporters. They all smiled quickly, then went straight to taking pictures and speaking into their recorders. A familiar woman walks through the door last. I have to hold back my sneer as she walked through the door.

"Hi, honey, is your father around?" The reporter asks, with a sickly sweet tone.

I know she knows I've seen her in my home. The audacity of her to come to my father's wedding knowing good and well she's the other woman is honestly shocking.

"All media will have to wait until the ceremony is over for questioning, ma'am." I keep my voice just as sweet as hers.

"I think I have VIP access,"

"I don't think so," I state again sharply, looking at the guest behind her. She gets the message and struts off with a huff. Her large heels sounding obnoxiously against the ground.

I don't like my father's mistress, I mean she was the one that ultimately ended my parents' marriage. However, my father is being just cruel letting his side chick strut around their wedding. Why even marry the girl if they're going to have problems?

Having me stand next to his mistress in a white dress is also cruel. I'd thought that the day I got a text from him. They wouldn't have any best men or bridesmaids. It was just going to be the couple and me up there.

But, again, who am I not to follow instructions

"How did I manage to get the prettiest girl here to be my date?" I turn at the voice.

"As my date are you ready to fix me food and pull out my chair? I don't expect to touch a single door while I'm here?" I joke.

"Oh, of course," He waves me off, "Only the best for my date."

I smile at the last few guests then make my way to the ceremony room. My father thinks he's funny as he sat Lucas' parents next to the head table and sat Lucas next to me at the head table. He would have to be alone for most of the ceremony, but from what he tells me that won't be a problem.

"I'm going to take you to your seat, then I'm going to head to the back, okay?"

"Can I get champagne?"

"You're underage," I shoot him a pointed look.

"Oh, please don't even start with that. I've seen you take a shot of Hennessy to the head,"

I'm going to ignore that comment because we have to spend the rest of the day together, but I will not forget about it. How come he saw me at the party and I didn't see him?

"Drink water," I state walking off to find where I was supposed to stand.

A worker waves me over from behind the large doubled doors. Once I get behind it, I have the makeup team on me and some other random ladies fix my hair and dress. Another random person lifts a water bottle to my lips telling me to drink. The people start to clear out as music starts playing in the ceremony room.

"Listen!" The wedding director yells into the busy hallway, "The order has changed, the walk will go: Mr. Beckette, Ms. Wilson, and then the final walk belongs to Miss Victoria Beckette!"

I blink at the short man.

That is the ultimate level of pettiness. Everyone knows that the bride has the last walk. That's so all attention and eyes are on her. This is her day, her time to shine, and my father just took that away from her.

I don't think the small speech I gave him caused him to make this decision. For whatever reason, he's giving this woman hell.

But I'll mind my business - for now.

Carol comes out of her dressing room. Her large dressmaking it hard to maneuver through the narrow hall. I offer her a tight-lipped smile and a nod. That's my best at trying to be cordial with my soon-to-be step-mother. She returns it with a small sigh and nods.

I do have to say, for someone to be marrying the love of their life today. She doesn't look too happy. I don't have many expectations for this marriage. I only hope for a quiet household after this. I now know that most likely won't be happening.

My father comes out of his dressing room. His eyes don't meet any of ours. He stands in front of the door wait for his cue. It was silent. All the people in the hall were quiet, still busy, but quiet.

When the doors open, his smile is bright and immediate. He feigns anxiousness as he walks down the aisle. Although I couldn't see the crowd from where I stood, I heard the claps and cameras clicking.

Carol positioned herself in front of the now-closed doors. I take the time to examine her. I'd like to see how she feels. She takes a deep breath, staring straight ahead into the door. I personally think she doesn't have any feelings in the relationship either. At least not anymore.

Why end one loveless marriage just to get into another one?

The doors open and again she walks, the only sound heard is the aw's of the crowd and the piano. From what I could see, she even faked a cry and crouched in the middle of the carpet.

Maybe they're perfect for each other

It was my turn in front of the door. I took a deep breath pushing any personal feelings away. I had to look content, happy even. The doors open slowly, bright lights blind me for half a second. Once all the white light clears, I can see all eyes on me. Cameras started clicking as soon as the doors open, but once I started walking I could hear the murmurs of the people around me.

"Look at her she looks so pretty!"

"She's all grown up."

"Such an elegant young lady, I can see why her father's proud."

The words that I heard were nice. I would make sure to speak to those people as soon as the ceremony was over. I kept my head straight, not wanting to make eye contact with anybody in the room. My father and his, almost no longer mistress, stood staring in each other's eyes affectionately. If I hadn't seen the behind the scenes I would think they were really in love. The sympathy that began to build for Carol slowly vanished as I saw the facade she put up as well.

Once I hit a certain point on the carpet, my father turns to me. A smile embraces his face and he helps me up the stairs to the elevated platform. He kisses me on the cheek and then whispers in my ear.

"Hug her."

I do as I'm told, playing nice for the cameras. After the fake family moment, I head to the side of her.

The priest starts with his long speech and I officially stop listening. Despite all the attention supposed to be on the couple, I keep feeling a pair of eyes on me. I subconsciously look towards the feeling. Lucas was staring right at me, he winks when he sees me looking back. I give him a soft smile, looking back at the priest.

I felt a sharp pain.

Lucas isn't who I wanted to be looking at right now. He's so nice to me, he makes me laugh, he's smart. So then what is the problem?

He doesn't get my heart racing like a certain pair of grey eyes. He doesn't occupy my mind as those grey eyes do. I don't ever yearn for his presence. As I stand next to a couple being married, I think of a wedding of my own. I'd be lying if I said the groom I saw was blank.

I do see someone as my groom - Lucas just isn't it.

Am I flirting with Lucas? Am I leading him on? I don't mean to, I definitely wouldn't want to hurt his feelings.

If I am leading him on, how do I lead him off? Is that even a thing? I'm overthinking, in fact, I'm confusing myself. Just a few weeks ago, I talked about cutting Axel off emotionally, and now I'm seeing him as my husband.

Here I have this nice, clean-cut boy as my date. When in a crowd full of people, he looks at me. Why can't I reciprocate the feelings?

Ugh, I'm so incredibly irritating

Do I even know what I want?

"I do."

<3

"The guests are free to eat and media may begin asking questions."

After a long freaking time of standing, I walk to the important people I needed to talk to. Once I had a good conversation with them, my night's obligations were finally over.

Our conversation consisted of me greeting them, then asking me how I feel, finally ending the conversation with a long statement of their business with my father. I almost forgot, them asking me if I was going to take over the business.

That would never happen, but they don't need to know that

I sat next to Lucas at the head table with a loud sigh, he slides a drink over to me with a smile.

"Looks like you've got this date thing down," I joke, sipping on the water.

"I thought you looked angelic walking down that aisle," He sways. "You stole the show,"

Axel calls me Angel; Lucas calls me angelic

"That wasn't my intention,"

"Of course it wasn't."

I look up at him, "Aren't you going to eat?"

"Are you?"

"No,"

"Then no,"

I chuckle slightly, "When I said I was high maintenance I didn't mean you had to starve yourself,"

"No need," He waves me off, "If my date doesn't eat, then I don't."

Again with the silence. I thought we were over this already. I try not to feel awkward about the silence and glance around. Lucas' voice picks up again, gratefully.

"How well do you know Axel Stone?"

"I don't know anybody too well,"

He gives me a pointed look, but I match his energy, "I try not to make assumptions about anybody,"

"Maybe that's where you fall flat,"

"I'm sorry?"

"He's bad news,"

"I've heard,"

"What would your father think about you hanging out with the heathen at school?"

"You see me look at him once in the library and suddenly I'm 'hanging out' with him?"

Lucas sighs, seeing the conversation's turn. I would normally calm myself down, but I'm so tired of people trying to tell me what's right and what's wrong. I'm growing rather tired of everyone's concern being in the wrong place. In a room full of facades and fake smiles, why are they worried about me?

"I hang out with you," I continue, "Why aren't you bad news?"

Lucas gives me another pointed look and laughs.

"What?" I ask, "You think because you can half-ass throw a ball, you're a good guy?"

I'm back to joking, again, pushing my personal feelings aside. I can't be myself around Lucas; I know that. I always feel like I have to watch my back. Another reason why I can't reciprocate any real feelings towards him.

"You're cool, Victoria Beckette, you know that?" He looks towards something behind me. I follow his gaze to the newly-wed couple walking to the table hand in hand after questioning. I look back towards Lucas.

"The coolest."

***

< Dress that is described >

~ Chapter 33 ~

A XEL'S POV

Lucas Saunters, huh?

He must be dumber than I thought if he thinks I haven't noticed his presence around Victoria. He always seems to be around. When I'm with her, he's normally not too far behind. I know Victoria hasn't noticed and I don't want to tell her - not yet.

It would be hard to believe if I just went and outright told her that he's following her, so until I get proof, I'll just have to spend more time with her.

Not that I'm complaining

"This fight - if you win - will get you fifteen thousand," Noah busts through the gym VIP doors.

"Dollars?"

We all look at Tyler. I slap him in the back of the head. This dude is the dumbest smart person I've ever met. He can give you all the elements on the periodic table, but ask how to screw in a lightbulb.

"Deal."

"Wait-"

"I don't care, deal."

"Listen-" Noah cuts sharply, "This dude isn't what you're used to. The bigger the money the higher the threat, you know that,"

"How bad can he be?" Now curious, Noah normally was for fighting anybody and everybody.

He sets a computer in front of me pressing play. The black screen blinks into an arena. A large man relentlessly beating into someone under him. I couldn't tell who the person under him was, his blood was the only thing I could see. The body lies motionless, yet the man on top kept throwing punches. Refs looked scared to get in the middle. Yelling and screams seemed to be the only sound.

Out of nowhere three cops came and pulled the bigger guy off of the motionless body. I can't see the man breathing, even after the larger guy is pulled off. While police were fighting with the bigger guy, paramedics flock to the body on the ground. With a few shakes of the head, that's when the video cuts off.

"The dude on the ground was Scott Taylor,"

"Was?"

"Kumar Williams beat him to death that day,"

"I'm pretty sure murder is like thirty years in jail and I don't think we're talking about fighting an elder here," Kaiden was right, why the hell isn't Kumar Williams in jail?

Believe me, I'm no angel, but murder is murder.

"There wasn't even a trial. Scott's wife and daughter buried him the next Friday and there were absolutely no consequences given to Kumar,"

"That only makes me want to fight him more,"

"He's an asshole - no doubt, but what I'm trying to say is that he has powerful people behind him. This guy might be more trouble than the money is worth,"

"I understand that, but bills are coming up and money is short. I don't know about you guys, but I can't go back to living with my father. I won't,"

"We're all running from something, Axel, but is the fight really worth your life? We've always made ends meet, this time isn't any different,"

"Exactly, that's why I'm taking the fight," I stand to go confirm the reservation with Romano. My hand was on the door before Kaiden spoke up.

"Think of Victoria,"

I froze. The reality of death hadn't crossed my mind until I thought of her. Sure, he was brutal, but so was I. I thought I could win, that's why I wanted to move forward with the fight. A flash of bright blue eyes shocked the idea right out of me.

Victoria

I have this burning urge to protect her at all times. I've felt that way since even before I found about her father and now that I know, it only makes it worse.

"Okay," I turn around, "We'll look at other options."

Tyler snorted, "Pussy,"

"Shut the hell the up."

<3

"Who burnt the fucking popcorn!" Athena yells from the kitchen. I roll my eyes.

"I bet three dollars it was Noah,"

"Oh, like you're any better," Noah scowls over at me, chucking a few black pieces of popcorn.

"Don't throw it! You'll make the whole house smell like that shit!"

We were back in our house, thinking of another way to come up with this month's rent. In all reality, our landlord is fed up with our shit. He's pushed the rent up to twenty-five hundred a month. If we were in better circumstances, we'd leave.

However, the truth is Stanley was the only one who would take in minors. All of us were fourteen when we ran away. A purple park bench used to be my go-to bed. I hate to admit it, but we were good on money until recently. After remembering where we came from we thought we were in a better place. Flashy cars blinded us and now we risk going back to how this started.

"I know we don't want to, but Marcos has been calling me for some time," Tyler added.

I shake my head, "I'm not going back to selling,"

"Maybe we don't have a choice,"

Marcos used to run with our group. We all ran away together. Just a couple of kids with some fucked up parents trying to make a living. One of the ways we got off the streets was selling drugs on some street corners. When we got enough money we bought this place and stopped selling.

Marcos never stopped though. I don't blame him, he was the best out of all of us with that. He worked his way all the way to the top of the game. All love to him though, we all do what we have to do. At the end of the day, he will always be like my brother.

"How's he doing though?" I ask.

"Good, a hell of a lot better than us,"

"That type of life gets old," Kaiden shakes his head, "The constant looking behind your back, come on guys we've all lived it. None of us were meant for it,"

No matter how much you sell, how much respect you get - you're still a bug. A mere gnat in a tarantula's world. There will always be someone above you. You will never matter. If you die, they'll have ten new guys to replace you in an hour. That fairytale of brotherhood is a lie.

They don't care about us.

They never did.

"I know- but it just makes me think-"

"Well quit thinking then," Kaiden cuts Tyler off.

"Keep brainstorming, in the meantime, Tyler call up Marcos. It would be nice to see our brother again," Tyler nods, picking up his phone and walking out of the room.

I mostly stepped in to stop the tension before it exploded. We always fight, but now wasn't the time. We had a small business, we sold weed at school. There is a large difference between what we do and what Marcos does. They sell shit that will get you in prison for life, not only drugs.

We beat people up that mess with us - they kill them.

That life isn't for me.

Tyler isn't entirely out of line for bringing up that option. I'm sure we could get more than enough money off of one night with Marco. The problem is we all know better than to think it stops at one night. The gang lets you go when the gang is done with you, not when you're done with the gang.

We left it once, we won't be so lucky the next time.

"We're not going to find a solution tonight so just chill out," Noah comments setting his feet up on the couch and turning the TV on.

"Boys are so dumb." Athena sits down on the floor munching on some black popcorn. I pop her in the back of the head, before turning my attention back on the TV screen.

"Wait! What is that?" Athena jumps randomly point at a title on the screen.

Mayor Beckette's Wonderful Wedding

He's not mayor yet

Noah clicks on it and the first thing I see is a beaming Victoria Beckette. She was wearing a white dress, most would think that's rude considering it's not her wedding. Honestly, let's be real, she would outshine the bride in a trash bag.

She was walking down the aisle with a small smile on her face. I had to blink twice. Something weird happened, like a vision. It was Victoria but in a wedding dress. She looked the same walking down the aisle only one thing was different - her smile.

In the weird flashback- vision- I just had her smile was a real one.

I shake my head - I'm just tired. I couldn't sleep now, though. She eyes had this magnetic nature to them, I couldn't look away. It made me feel bad that I couldn't be there to tell her how pretty she was.

I can't help but chuckle to myself, she has no idea how pretty she is.

I watched her dazed look as she stood next to the bride, her new stepmother, whoever she was. Time seemed to run together and slow at the same time. Before I knew it she was walking to the head table.

Then, whatever haze ended as I saw who sat next to her seat at the head table.

Lucas - motherfucking - Saunters

He was sitting at the head table, next to her father. I bet he doesn't even know how she feels. I bet he doesn't even care to ask.

I was furious beyond belief. When I've ever brought up Saunters she always seems uninterested. So what the hell happened to make her introduce him to her father-

I couldn't be mad, she did see me, buddy-buddy, with her best friend. However, we fought and she never gave me a chance to explain. She didn't even seem to care.

Maybe she's not into me - The thought had never crossed my mind before, but that wasn't a very fair assumption because I never think when it comes to her.

I snatch the remote from Noah, turning off the TV.

"The fights on."

~ Chapter 34 ~

I woke up to a text from my father. It only stated that he and my new stepmother weren't going to be home for a long time. I assume that he's talking about some sort of honeymoon. I am not in the least bit upset about having the house to myself.

I also woke up to a second text. That one was from Athena saying that I needed to talk to Axel. There was no other context than that, but I didn't really need any. I think I have a basic idea of why Axel might be upset.

However, he has no room to be too upset. I hadn't even mentioned another word about what happened with him and Olivia at the side of the school. I had a come to Jesus moment with myself and realized that I'm still not over that. I didn't even question him about it.

The worst part is that I know he knows he's wrong for that.

With a deep sigh, I text Athena asking where he is, and roll out of bed. Maybe I would even make myself a nice breakfast now that I have the whole house to myself. I might just try hanging out in other rooms besides my room.

After my extremely long and hot shower, I put on something cute and trotted downstairs. I can't even remember the last time I cooked something in my kitchen. I do, however, remember that one reason I don't cook is that I'm not very good at it.

A good thirty minutes pass and I realize that the fridge is completely empty besides some old juice and last year's Easter eggs. Does Carol not cook for my father? What do they eat? What do I eat?

I drink the rest of the stale juice and head to my car. Athena said that Axel was at the gym preparing for his next fight, so the gym it is.

Could Axel really have seen the recording of the wedding? That just doesn't really seem like the type of thing he would watch. I give up on being stubborn and decide to call Athena. I should at least try and understand what I'm walking into.

"Good morning, Angel," She sings into the phone.

"Athena..."

"I- I feel like it's not my place to tell you. You know I love you, so it's not bad," She cuts herself off with a sigh, "We just feel like you're the only person that can talk him out of this,"

"We?"

"Yes, me and the guys,"

"Okay, what is he trying to do?"

"It would be more effective if he explained it to you,"

Well, this has been the most unhelpful conversation I've ever had in my entire life

"Will you guys be at the gym?"

"No, it's closed. My father let Axel in because he knows what he's training for,"

"So basically everyone knows what going on except me?" I ask turning into the gym parking lot.

There was no one here. The only vehicle in the parking lot was a pretty black bike. Both my heart and head were pounding inside of me. Why the hell am I so nervous? I did nothing wrong. It wasn't even my choice to go with Lucas. I would've rather taken Axel as my date-

I would never tell him that though

"Actually, yes," Her voice quips into my speakers.

"Alright, I love you," I smile lightly, "Tell my parents I want purple flowers at my funeral,"

"I love you more," She laughs.

Before I shut off the call she speaks up again, "Vic, please don't let him do anything stupid. We might not show it often, but we really care about him,"

My heart melts inside my chest - I care about him too.

"Of course."

I turn my car off and stalk towards the gym doors. The sound of a punching welcomes me into the hot building. Axel's back was facing me, but he knew I was here. I set my stuff down still standing by the benches. I wanted to give him some space. I didn't know exactly how he was feeling and I hadn't really planned on getting into an explosive argument today.

Axel's shirtless, sweaty back was hypnotizing. His movements were fluent; they were controlled, yet powerful. The most important part was that he looked so damn good while doing it.

"Axel..."

My voice rang through the empty gym. Bouncing off of unused equipment. Dancing right into his ears. However, he kept punching. If I didn't know any better I'd say his punches got a little sloppy at the sound of my voice.

I took a few steps closer, this time I could see his face.

"You're going to ignore me? That's fine, but I'm not leaving," I spoke again still no reaction from him.

"Come on, Axel," I let out a breathy whine, "Can I at least know what I did wrong? And can you tell me why Athena is worried about you?"

"Is that why you came? Because Athena called you?" He stopped punching altogether. In the same motion, he turns fully toward me. His breath heavy and uneven. The smoke coming from his ears was imaginary but still very much there.

"Why the hell else would I come? I wouldn't even know you had a problem with me if I didn't get her text," I exasperated, "You sure didn't let me know,"

"Whatever, Victoria."

He begins to walk away and I contemplate, for a small moment, on letting him go. The smart part of me knows that it's not a good idea to just let him walk away. The petulant side of me curls into a ball at the thought of chasing after him. Despite him being mad at me, Athena asked me to stop him from doing something stupid. I'm going to at least try and find out what that is.

"Absolutely not," I step in front of him, "I'm not the girls you're used to dealing with. You don't get to just walk away. I'm as stubborn as you, motherfucker, we can do this all day,"

"He's bad - fucking - news, yet you insist on keeping him around" He spits, "Don't act like you don't know,"

"Oh, I know, but I want to hear it from you,"

He shakes his head, gently pushing past me. I close my eyes for a moment. When dealing with Axel it always brings my emotions to their complete capacity. He made everything so difficult. Nothing was normal with him.

How can someone that brings me so much happiness, bring me so much distress?

"My father asked him," I start, begrudgingly, "The Saunters are close business partners with my family. If that wasn't bad enough, my father didn't tell me. Lucas let it slip to me in the library,"

Recognization glazed Axel's expression. "Yes, the day you decided to glare at us from across the room,"

He snorts.

"I didn't think you would care, so I didn't mention it,"

He scoffs, "You're so oblivious,"

"Oblivious to what, Axel? Every time we're on a good page one of us fucks it up and we're back to hating each other. We take a step forward only to take five steps back. Nothing is ever good enough for you!"

"Do I not give you the same energy back? Every time you need me, I'm there,"

"So what do you want from me, Axel? What are we doing here?"

"How do you want me to answer that?"

At this point, I hadn't even noticed the liquid gathering behind my eyes. Axel was facing me, his body shaking, clenching, and unclenching his jaw.

"How do you want me to answer that?" My voice was softer now as I retort the question. I don't know what I was expecting to hear, but that absolutely was not it. "I think you just did,"

"Prince-"

"Axel, don't you fucking dare," I jabbed at his chest.

"This," I gesture between the two of our bodies, "Obviously isn't going to work, you need to find out what you want and you need to find out fast,"

"I should be asking you the same thing," He grabbed my hand, not in a violent way. I don't know what the gesture was supposed to do, but I do know that even when I'm at my angriest with him. My body still responds to his touch.

"You already know," I yank my hand away from him, "That's why you treat me like this, right?"

"What-"

"You make a few cute gestures. You get to know my home life, maybe flirt a little bit in between that. Then you throw everything back into my face," I roughly wipe whatever tears fell from my eyes, "Then for the final - fucking - finale, you kiss my best friend!"

It slipped, through my blinding anger, it slipped.

"You never even asked what happened,"

"Yeah, because I have eyes,"

"I didn't kiss her,"

"I don't care," I retort, "I don't care because you can kiss whoever you want to, you can fuck whoever you want. Axel Stone, it has nothing to do with me- you have nothing to do with me-"

Within seconds his lips were enclosed on mine. Before I could even think about what was happening I was kissing him back. It was as if our bodies were on the same wavelength and our minds were the ones fighting.

He tasted sweet, addicting even. He was a drug in human form, I knew that before kissing him though. Axel hooked his hands under my thighs lifting me up, slamming me against the cement wall. The kiss was rough and demanding. It wasn't a fight of dominance it was just a fight of hunger. He was trying to taste more of me and vice versa.

I was breathing him in, never wanting to be so completely embraced by him. I couldn't even remember what we were arguing about or what I was supposed to ask him. As his hands ran over my body all I could think about was him.

His lips melted into mine with ease. I have no idea how long we were in our position. Time seemed to be a nonfactor in his arms. Forever and now was all that was on my mind.

I eventually snapped out of whatever daze I had been in and pulled back. Any words I'd manage to think of is erased from my mind as I saw the state I left him in. His hair disheveled and lips puffy. His grey eyes still dilated in hunger.

"My God," He gasped, "You're fun to kiss."

I couldn't manage to get anything out. I couldn't even manage to move. All I could do is stare at him wide-eyed.

Well, that just made things a lot more complicated

~ Chapter 35 ~

My heart was still racing.

It's been racing since I kissed him. It raced when I stumbled out of the gym. It continued to race as I drove my car straight home. I was too frazzled to even remember why I'd gone to the gym in the first place.

Nothing could take the cheek-hurting smile that was plastered on my face. Well, that was until I woke up without a single text from a certain grey-eyed boy. All Sunday I waited for a single text, just something - anything.

I was given nothing.

I can't explain in words what I was expecting from him. I just wanted some clarification, maybe? Something to tell me that kissing him wasn't a mistake. It sure didn't feel like a mistake. I might be expecting too much from him. I'm almost positive I'm not the only girl he's ever kissed. SO a kiss could mean nothing.

I pull up to the school, eyes already set on the pretty black bike parked across the lot. I hop out of my car making sure to not even look their way. Instead, I smile widely at the sight of Mia walking towards the school doors.

I feel his eyes burn at my back. However, I refused to turn around. I think I've given Axel Stone the wrong impression of myself. I most definitely wasn't wrapped around his finger. If he wasn't going to make an effort to talk to me, I wouldn't go out of my way either.

I could play his game a hundred times better than he could

"Mia!"

She turns around with a smile, "Hey! I was just about to call you,"

"When is Christmas break again?'

"It's already passed," She laughs.

"Ugh, right."

We walk arm in arm into the building. Finding some acquaintances to talk to, passing the time. When the large doors slammed open, I refused to look. When I heard the boots hit the tile flooring, I refused to pause my conversation. Then, against my internal wishes, the boots walk right past me.

"The sexual tension is suffocating,"

I look towards Mia, frowning.

"With who?"

"You, bitch," She snorts, "You and Mr. Badboy,"

"Oh, hush," I wave her away, "We didn't even look at each other,"

"You didn't look at him, but he definitely looked at you. He looks mad, what did you do to him?"

"Isn't he always mad?"

Now, what sense does that make? I could, again, be taking this completely out of proportion. Is a text after a kiss too much to ask? Maybe I'm being unfair, he's not obligated to text me first. For all I know he might've been sitting right next to the phone waiting for me to text him.

He most definitely wasn't doing that.

RING

"Meet me at lunch?"

"Meet at lunch."

<3

We had a substitute teacher for french this fine morning. The work she left, was that we work in our groups for some random worksheet. I, of course, was partnered with Lucas. However, the sub was pretty cool, and let us sit outside to do our work.

It was a wonderful day after all.

However, there was a down to sitting outside, there always is. Axel Stone happened to be skipping class outside as well. This time when I saw him, we did make eye contact. I only broke it when Lucas asked a question.

I automatically felt bad, I'd just told Axel that I wanted nothing with Lucas, and here I am sitting outside with him. I know I was just thinking about 'playing Axel's game' but hurting his feelings was never in the equation.

By the time we'd finished our worksheet, Axel had gone through three cigarettes. He didn't say a word but the boys must've sensed his mood and soon looked over at me too.

"He's bad news you know,"

"Funny," I glance in Axel's direction again, "He said the same thing about you,"

"Listen, Victoria," Lucas moves himself to sit right next to me, "You're not the only girl that thinks she can change a boy. I just want to let you know that there's other options,"

Who said I wanted to change him?

"What's the other option, Lucas?"

He doesn't make eye contact, looking away. Lucas Saunters had my complete attention now. I just hope he's not about to suggest what I think he's about to suggest. I think Lucas is a great guy, but he's not what I want. I can't even sit here and pretend.

"Can't you see the influence he's has on you?" Lucas was getting fiery, "He's got you skipping class, going to illegal fights, drag racing,"

"And who the hell told you that?"

"People talk-"

"Bullshit," I cut him off, standing up, "Do you think I'm dumb Lucas? That I can't connect the dots?"

"Victoria, that's- I didn't mean to say that-"

"Of course you didn't," I snarl, "Now, tell me is my father paying you, or do you do this for fun?"

"This isn't where I planned on taking this conversation," He pauses, "Victoria, I think you're amazing. Beautiful, smart, funny-"

"I haven't told you a single joke,"

"You didn't have to,"

"Did you watch me shower too? Or do you have boundaries?"

"No, I haven't gotten to that yet,"

"You think you're funny?" I raise a brow.

"What's so different? Do you think he wasn't watching you too? Tell me, Victoria, why do you think he's taken an interest in you all of a sudden?"

"Right, because I can't just pull a guy with my personality,"

"I know you're not stupid Victoria. Axel Stone likes illegal activities and your father is the only one in the state in his way. He doesn't give a fuck about you,"

Lucas grabs my arm, pulling it to his chest. His grab wasn't like Axel's. He was hurting me. I don't think I've ever seen Lucas angry. I can't even understand why he's the one upset with me. I'm confused beyond belief on how this escalated so fast.

I rip my arm away from him, turning to run. I, mentally, didn't know where I was going, but it looks my body did.

I ran, they all were looking, but I didn't care - I ran to him.

I ran in the opposite direction of Lucas. A body meeting me halfway. I instantly wrapped my arms around him, he took no time doing the same. I could hear the other boys run past us towards Lucas.

"Axel- I'm sorry-"

"Shhh," He holds me tighter, "It's alright,"

"You're an idiot. A cute idiot, but still an idiot,"

"He was just my French partner, I didn't even pick him," I continued to rant.

"Princess, just calm down, it doesn't matter."

The only thing I could feel was relief. I have to say, out of all the ways I could've seen that conversation going. That was not one of them. Lucas hadn't even hinted to me that he had a quick-tempered side. Truthfully, I know as much about Lucas has me knows about me, or as much as he thinks he knows about me.

"Come on, let's go," I shake myself off.

"Alright, where?"

"Anywhere but here, please."